BULL'S-EYE

Bolan sprayed the wreckage with a full clip of thirty-caliber steeljackets, dropped a medal on the ground beside it, and walked back to check the guys who'd been blasted clear of the grenaded car.

The first one he reached was obviously dead, his face a pulp, clothing in flames.

The other was twisted around a shotgun—big guy, tough-looking, but hardly more than a kid.

And he was alive . . . momentarily. Bolan could not figure out why. Half his chest was missing and the cavity was awash with bubbling blood; he could even see the heart pumping. One eye only was open, and that eye was watching Mack Bolan.

He said, "Sorry, kid," and extended the chattergun in a one-hand hold. Bolan pumped a short burst from the fresh clip into him, hastening the inevitable process already set in motion.

He dropped a bull's-eye cross atop that tragedy and muttered, "It was a hard world, kid. You can go home now. Better luck next time out.

The Executioner Series

the EXECUTIONER
ST. LOUIS SHOWDOWN

by Don Pendleton

PINNACLE BOOKS • NEW YORK CITY

This is a work of fiction. All the characters and events portrayed in this book are fictional, and any resemblance to real people or incidents is purely coincidental.

THE EXECUTIONER: ST. LOUIS SHOWDOWN

Copyright © 1975 by Pinnacle Books, Inc.

An original Pinnacle Books edition, published for the first time anywhere.

ISBN: 0-523-00687-X

First printing, October 1975

Cover illustration by Gil Cohen

Printed in the United States of America

PINNACLE BOOKS, INC.
275 Madison Avenue
New York, N.Y. 10016

This book is dedicated to the hellgrounds—
and to all who labor there in high ideals,
however vainly.

dp

The mind is its own place,
and in itself
Can make a heaven of Hell,
a hell of Heaven.
　—JOHN MILTON *(Paradise Lost)*

This is where the world is made—out here in Hell. But there is no sense to Hell when there are no people in Heaven. Some of us must choose Hell, some Heaven. I have made my choice. And I intend to rule this place if I can, if only to make some sense of it!
　—MACK BOLAN (his War Journal)

PROLOGUE

In the war zones of Southeast Asia his government had given him the code name The Executioner. Enemy commands referred to him as "that devil"—and put a price on his head. Others in that same war zone, however, called him Sergeant Mercy, and many sick and terrorized villagers of that bloodied land owed their lives to this committed young man who walked those trails of hell with death in one hand and compassion in the other.

Mack Bolan was a penetration specialist, leader of an elite group known officially as Able Team. Their business was espionage, sabotage, demoralization, death—in a highly personal reference. These jungle fighters lived off the land and ranged far and wide through enemy territories, usually totally isolated from their own forces, often separated from one another, and operating independently—self-sufficient, self-commanding, waging war and surviving through sheer wit and instinct.

Bolan himself was generally regarded by his peers as the master at the game. He was a phenomenal marksman, a cool and patient warrior, a nerveless death machine with unerring instincts and awesome determination. His official kills of enemy bigwigs had approached the one-hundred mark, and his exploits had become legendary in every military enclave when The Executioner was suddenly called home on humanitarian leave.

His entire family had become victims of another sort of war.

Mack Bolan never returned to the jungles of Southeast Asia. Instead, he brought them home with him, buried his own beloved dead, and launched his personal war against "the greater enemy" at home.

Never had a man so qualified been faced with a challenge so awesome.

Mack Bolan, The Executioner, declared war on the Mafia. It was a hopeless sort of war—illegal, immoral, impossible—but the resourceful and determined sergeant from Able Team was waging it with unparalleled commitment and dedication—and it was even beginning to appear that he might succeed where armies of police had failed.

He had carried the fight to the enemy and survived more than twenty pitched battles, employing a mixture of jungle wiles and blitzkrieg assaults which usually left the enemy in stunned disarray and with heavy losses. The odds remained almost the same, however—and Bolan realized that he was fighting a beast which grew new heads and limbs as fast as he could hack them off.

He was in constant jeopardy, also, from a pyramiding police reaction to his illegal crusade. Bolan himself was now the "most wanted criminal" in America, and his every known move was instantly flashed to law enforcement agencies throughout the free world.

It was also a well-known fact that Bolan's head would make an instant millionaire of the lucky gunman who could deliver it to the desperate men who ruled *La Cosa Nostra*; such was the aggregate payoff of a dozen "open contracts" issued on Mack Bolan's life—and the scramble of the bounty hunters became wilder with every day that the formidable one-man army remained alive. Any punk who could scrape up the price of a Saturday-night special was a potential enemy and a constant threat to this man whose precarious path of life became, of grim necessity, even narrower and lonelier.

A few trusted and scattered friends remained to offer covert assistance to the war and unyielding concern for the man, but Bolan shunned even these few contacts to the greatest possible degree. He was a walking disaster and knew it; one day he would be pulled down, and he had no desire to involve others in his unavoidable fate.

There were times, though, when Bolan felt that the dictates of the moment outweighed the cautions—when the stakes were too high to be affected by personal considerations. And these were the circumstances that precipitated the St. Louis Showdown.

His old Able Team partner and Death Squad survivor, Rosario (the Politician) Blancanales, had spotted the play in Missouri and sent word to perhaps the one man in the world who could add a meaningful dimension to the game. The flash had not come as a particularly surprising development to Bolan. He had known for some time of ambitious movements in the Show Me State. But he had been wary of St. Louis. A steady infusion of hardline torpedoes had been stiffening the area ever since the Texas hit. There had been noises to the effect that Jerry Ciglia's St. Louis boys were the nucleus of a new, national stop-Bolan effort, and there had been various indications from other quarters to support that notion. Bolan had recently tangled with Ciglia—but in another territory and with the advantage on Bolan's side. The whole Missouri thing could be a trap

3

play designed to lure him into a situation where all the advantage would be on the other side.

Mack Bolan was not a "wild-ass warrior"—as some seemed to believe. He was a cautious and a wary one, and he had remained alive thus far because of that fact. He responded to the SOS from St. Louis not with a gung-ho spirit but rather with a sigh of resignation. A showdown at St. Louis had become inevitable. Bolan was the sort of man who could face the inevitable. He went. But not, he hoped, as prey. He went as The Executioner to do a job which could no longer be avoided.

Such was the situation on that brooding spring night when a sleek GMC motor home left Interstate 270 north of St. Louis and climbed the high ground to a bluff overlooking the night glow of the riverside city. Bolan sent his warwagon nosing into the parking area of a Holiday Inn and pulled into the overlook. Moments later another vehicle eased in beside him. A dark, strongly built man in casual dress moved quickly to the van and stepped inside. The greeting between the two old friends was warm but subdued.

"You're looking great," Bolan said with a tight smile.

"You too," Blancanales replied. "I was about to give you up. I been camped up here for two nights."

"I know," Bolan said, smiling. "I've been looking you over for two nights."

The two men chuckled. The dark one said, "I could've guessed it. I didn't see you ... but, man, I could *feel* you. Where were you?"

Bolan's steely blue gaze flicked toward the lights of the motel. "Been here most the time. Checked in Wednesday. Left the warwagon parked in Burke City while I reconned the situation here."

"Am I clean?" Blancanales grunted.

Bolan grinned. "I wouldn't be here if you weren't. So what's with the SOS?"

The Politician scowled as he replied, "They're getting ready to take over this town. They could do it, too—they've got the kicker. And there's visions of a Capone-era Chicago transplanted to old Saint Louie. Your buddy Ciglia is the guy with the franchise."

"What's the kicker?" Bolan asked quietly.

"Curious situation here, Sarge. The city has no control over its own police department. State law. The commissioners are appointed by the governor."

Bolan frowned. "That's the kicker?"

"That's it. Does the name Newman—Chuck Newman—mean anything to you?"

"No," Bolan replied, cocking his head thoughtfully. "Should it?"

"I thought maybe—I knew the guy in 'Nam. Special forces—he was in the pacification program. Well he's in politics here, now. Running for governor. Looks like he'll make it, too, especially now that, uh . . ."

"The mob's behind him?"

"In a backhanded sort of way, yeah. Chuck didn't invite them in. They just horned in, planning to ride the poor guy right into the state house."

Bolan sighed. "What do they have on him?"

Blancanales dropped his eyes and fidgeted. "His wife. She has, uh, past indiscretions."

"The guy should withdraw," Bolan decided coldly.

"He wants that office awfully bad, Sarge. Besides, they won't let him out. They're holding this stuff over his head like a time bomb. Either he plays ball or the bomb goes off."

"Must be quite a bomb," Bolan observed sourly.

"It is. The lady was a porn queen—back when all that stuff was strictly underground. It's been so long ago—well, she thought the past was dead and buried. Then Ciglia turns up with half a dozen of those old films under his wing. Look—Chuck knew all about that stuff when he married her. He's that kind of guy—he married her for what she was, not what she'd

5

once been. Now they have a couple of nice kids, social position—ahhh hell, Sarge, you know the routine. Ciglia says he'll release the films into the legitimate porn outlets unless Newman dances to his tune. You know what that would do to that lady, those kids—forget about the political ambitions."

Bolan said, "Yeah, that's quite a kicker. I suppose Ciglia also already has his own police commissioner picked out for St. Louis."

"Sure. And that's only the beginning."

"Is Newman a client of Able Group?" Bolan inquired.

"Yeah. He learned about us via the New Orleans publicity. Contacted me a couple of weeks ago. Wants me to get those damned films. Hell. It's an impossible assignment, Sarge. Except, maybe, unless . . ."

"You didn't call me over here for that," Bolan said.

The Politician grinned. "Not really. But I've got the town wired now. And I know just how bad the general situation is—forgetting Newman's personal problems. I thought you'd be interested. And I thought, maybe, in the fallout . . ."

Bolan growled, "Yeah."

And sure, he was very interested. This town should have been on his hit parade long before now.

He sighed and told his old partner, "Okay, Pol—I'll want a full briefing. I want everything you've got. Then I want Able Group to pull out and remain clear—at least until all the pieces have settled."

Blancanales smiled sourly and fidgeted as he replied, "Well, uh, that, uh . . ."

Bolan sighed again, heavily, and asked, "Just how deep in are you?"

"Clear up to Toni's neck, I'm afraid," the Pol replied with a grimace. "She's been playing the inside game with Ciglia. No contact since Monday." He raised his hands to shoulder level and slowly lowered them.

"Gadgets and I have been out of our heads trying to get a line on her."

Bolan said, "Well, dammit, Pol. You should have told me that when——"

"It wasn't a problem then. I've had no chance to tell you, 'til now."

Bolan ran a hand across his forehead and gazed stonily upon the metropolitan sprawl which numbered more than two million inhabitants and nearly three thousand square miles. Toni was the Pol's kid sister and a licensed investigator with Able Group, the detective agency chartered by Blancanales and Gadgets Schwarz in the wake of the San Diego Siege. Bolan had met Toni for the first time during the battle for New Orleans, and a rather special thing had developed between the two.

Yeah, a very special thing.

And now she was somewhere out there in that no man's land where only the brave and the bold survived, and then only the very best of those.

"Okay," he said quietly.

No further words were necessary to explain his decision. It was, Blancanales knew, going to be a hell of a hot time for the old steamboat city.

1: FROM THE TOP

Mack Bolan was starting at the top in St. Louis. A couple hours of darkness remained of the night when the wraithlike figure dropped quietly over the wall surrounding a crumbling estate in an exclusive neighborhood on St. Louis' west side. He was outfitted in night-black combat garb. The chillingly silent Beretta Belle rode head-weapon position beneath his left arm; the impressive .44 AutoMag occupied the thunder spot at the right hip. A ready belt of personal munitions crossed the chest. Nylon garrotes and pencil-diameter stilettos were slit-pocketed onto the outer calf of each leg.

There had been no time for a daylight reconnoiter of the target. He was moving entirely on combat instincts as he silently crossed the fifty yards of rear lawn to the shadows of the three-story house.

The place belonged to Arturo (Little Artie) Giamba, titular head of the St. Louis mob for many years. Giamba was one of the old guard, an aging nickle-and-dimer of little imagination and limited ambitions

9

who had been content to sit atop a crumbling empire and watch it fade away in concert with his own life.

The Giamba Family was a poor cousin in the national alliance of organized crime and was not even represented on the ruling council, *La Commissione*.

But things were changing.

Bolan needed to discover just how far the change had gone. According to intelligence sources, Jerry Ciglia had been sent down by New York to "revitalize" the territory, bringing an army of torpedoes with him. Shortly thereafter, Giambia had dropped from view. Underworld rumors of his fate covered the full range from execution to genteel exile in a Latin American republic. Ciglia himself had been in rather low profile in the area since his arrival, but it was known that he had set up his headquarters in the old Giamba mansion.

So, yeah, Bolan was starting at the top in St. Louis. If he should luck onto Ciglia clean, he'd take the guy with the first shot of the battle. And it was too bad, Bolan was thinking as he loped across that no man's land between wall and house, that he hadn't wasted the guy on that golf green down on the Gulf Coast. Maybe all this would be unnecessary, now. It had been a different game, then, of course. Ciglia had been a mere pawn in that fight. So now he was the king . . . and that was the way things went in Mack Bolan's world. It was a war of attrition that paved the highway to hell with broken bodies and mortgaged souls, and yet there never seemed to be any attrition in the ranks of the enemy. Like targets in a shooting gallery, knock one down and another pops up in its place—on and on, endlessly, clear to hell's gates. So sure, forget the what-ifs; the name of the king meant not a damned thing. If it were not Ciglia then it would be someone else. It was not the man that mattered, it was the office—and Mack Bolan had come to St. Louis to slay an idea, not a man. Men were going to die, for damn sure, but only because there was no other way to get rid of the idea.

But Jerry Ciglia would not take top honors as the first to die in this battle. An indolent shape detached itself from the shadows at the rear of the house as Bolan approached and a lazy, unconcerned voice drawled, "Who's that?"

The Beretta chugged a pencil of flame in response, but the guy never heard the whispering death that blew across that twenty-foot range to snap him back and punch him over, dead before the fall.

Bolan dropped a medal on the dead soldier's chest as he stepped across the mess and went on around the side of the house to check out the forward area. He found another yardman there, near the vehicle gate, and dropped him just as quietly, then returned to the building with no lost motion.

Knowing hands found the telephone cable and cut it. Several heartbeats later, he was on the rear service porch—a glassed-in affair with laundry tubs and a hodgepodge of appliances. He located the main power panel there and disabled it.

A quick kick in a vital spot sent the kitchen door creaking inward, and he was inside—pencil flash in hand and moving swiftly.

Just beyond a swinging door lay the dining room, and seated there in the dark over an interrupted game of solitaire was a heavy guy in shirt-sleeves and bulging shoulder holster.

Bolan sent the beam directly into the guy's eyes and kept on moving.

"What happened to the lights?" the guy grumbled, holding a card to his eyes to shield them from the flashlight beam.

"I put them out," Bolan replied quietly—then the big silver thundergun was muzzle-up to the guy's nose and no further explanation was necessary.

11

"Easy, easy," the guy croaked. "Anything you say, eh?"

Bolan deposited the flashlight on the table and disarmed the houseman, then he dropped a bull's-eye cross into the center of the solitaire spread.

The guy groaned and his facial muscles tightened, eyes bulging at the little medal; otherwise he was a marble statue.

Bolan coldly told him, "I guess it's you and me, baby. You've got about a heartbeat to decide how long it'll stay that way."

"Name it," the houseman replied quickly, no decision necessary.

"Who's here?"

"Jerry and a broad, master suite, top of the stairs, second floor. His two shadows across the hall. Two boys on outside detail. Another boy on the third floor with the old man. That's it."

"So far, so good," Bolan said in those icy tones reserved for the living dead. "Who're you?"

The guy's eyes clouded. At a moment such as this, in a world such as this, identity could be a highly important thing. "I'm Steve Rocco," he said, sighing.

"Out of Chicago," Bolan decided.

"Yeah. You, uh, I think met my brother Benny once."

"Your *late* brother Benny," Bolan reminded.

"Yeah, well—you take your paycheck and your own chances, I guess. I ain't holding no—"

"You're holding your life in your own hands, Rocco. I hope you're not a butterfingers."

"I can be very careful," the guy said very soberly.

"What's Ciglia doing to the old man?"

"Starving 'im, I guess. Nothing goes up there but bread and water, and not much of that."

"Why?"

Rocco shrugged beefy shoulders. "Hell, I'm just one of the troops. They don't let me in on their secrets."

Bolan freed a concussion grenade from his ready belt and rolled it into the next room. Rocco's startled gaze leapt after it, swiveling him about in the chair as he momentarily forgot all else.

It was a short fuse. The explosion shook the room and sent a turret of flame up the stairwell.

Rocco staggered from the chair with a dazed, "Jeez! . . ."

"Here's your life. Careful," Bolan declared coldly. "Something just blew up. We've got a fire. They better not chance the stairs. Out the windows, and damn quick."

The guy nodded understandingly and swallowed a heavy lump which had formed in his throat.

A yell floated down from the upper level as doors opened up there amid a hubbub of confusion. Then Jerry Ciglia's sleep-thickened bawl: "Stevie! What the hell is—"

"Something blew up!" the houseman screamed back. "The joint's on fire!"

"The lights!" Ciglia yelled. "What the hell's wrong with the lights?"

"Everything's out, boss," Rocco screamed. "Don't try them stairs! Get outta there, *quick*!"

Bolan had rolled another grenade toward the stairs, the explosion coming one beat behind the houseman's warning and sending another tower of flames and smoke whoofing up the stairwell.

There was no further comment from above. Bolan told his man, "This is the sweetest thing I can do for you, Rocco," as he conked him with the butt of the AutoMag. He left the guy lying there and swiftly ascended the stairs. Two steps along the dark and smoky upstairs hallway he collided with soft warm flesh and instinctively gathered it in, shutting off a feminine gasp with a quiet warning.

"*You*!" she exclaimed in a shocked whisper.

"Who else? Where's your buddy?"

"I believe he just dived out the window. Mack—Mr. Giamba is locked into the attic room. I was just headed—"

"I'll get him. You beat it down the stairs and straight out the rear. Wait for me on the other side of the wall."

"Well, wait—*no*! I've got the inside track here! I'm not going to—"

"Toni, dammit, trust me and beat it! *Now*!"

She moved away from him without another word and Bolan followed the bannister on around and went up the stairs to the floor above. It was no more than a one-room garret with a door set almost into the landing at the top of the stairs.

That door was open, now, and there were no sounds of life within. Bolan chanced the flashlight and found Little Artie Giamba lying face down on the floor halfway between the bed and an open window. A rope-ladder fire escape dangled there. The guard had left the weakened old man to shift for himself.

Some world, Bolan's was.

He hoisted the pajama-clad figure to his shoulder in a fireman's carry, then made quick tracks out of there.

And, yeah, he was starting at the top in St. Louis. This old man was the mission goal, and it was a first for Mack Bolan. It was a rescue mission . . . for a *capo*.

2: THIS OLD MAN

The new boss of St. Louis was hobbling about the darkened and battered interior of his headquarters in his underwear, favoring a painful ankle and checking the damage with a flashlight—and he was mad as hell.

The most incredible part was that more damage had not been done. A couple of windows were blown out, the floor around the stairwell and the lower few steps were badly splintered,-paint blistered from walls and scorched woodwork—but that was about the extent of it.

Ciglia promised Nate Palmieri, his chief tagman, "I catch the wise guy threw those firecrackers, I'm going to shove one up his ass and personally light the fuse."

Palmieri grunted an agreement with that idea, then observed, "It could have been a lot worse, Jerry. Let's count blessings, for now. I better go out to the gate and tell Jonesy to stay locked up. One of our good neighbors may have called for cops or firemen."

"Right, we don't need any of that," the boss agreed.

15

He turned to the other bodyguard and asked, "How's Stevie?"

"Coming around," was the reply.

The unconscious houseman had been carried to a couch and was getting the wet towel treatment from Jake Rio.

"Go see about the lights," Ciglia ordered brusquely.

A lamp in the dining room came on before the bodyguard could react to that command. Seconds later, a fourth man hurried into the blast zone. This was Homer Gallardo, the upstairs man. He reported, "The main power bus had been pulled. Some smart bastard . . ."

"He cut the phones, too," Ciglia growled. "Find it and fix it."

Gallardo nodded, said, "probably out at the box," and hurried on toward the front of the house.

Steve Rocco groaned and tried to raise himself upright.

Ciglia limped over there, gave his houseman a penetrating gaze, and said, "Easy, Stevie. You took a bad hit there. Just lay still for a minute. You're going to have a hell of a headache. What happened here?"

Rocco groaned again and gave his boss a glassy stare. "Hell, I don't know," he replied groggily.

"Well, try and think about it. You yelled 'fire'. There was a couple of explosions, some kind of bombs. Did you see anybody?"

Rocco's eyes fluttered and closed. "I guess I just panicked, boss. I didn't see a thing but flames shooting up the stairs."

"Okay, just lie there and get your head together," Ciglia growled. "Maybe it'll come to you."

The bodyguard coiled the wet towel about Rocco's face and went into the dining room. He returned quickly, bouncing a small object in the palm of his

16

hand. "You gotta see this, boss," he announced in a tightening voice, handing the object over for inspection.

Ciglia froze there for a moment in the light from the open doorway, then he spun quickly into the comfort of darkness and commanded, "Kill that light!"

The bodyguard lunged into the dining room and sent the lamp flying off the table and into the wall with a crash. Only a thin sliver of light now shone through the swinging door from the kitchen.

"Where'd you find that goddamned thing?" Ciglia called over in a guarded voice.

"On the table," Rio replied.

"Have you seen Jonesy or Huck since the blast?"

"No, boss. I just started wondering about that."

"Well, stop wondering. Get out back and take a look around for Huck. And be careful."

The tagman moved out without another word.

Steve Rocco groaned something and Ciglia furiously shushed him.

Moments later, cautious steps moved across the front porch, then the door cracked open and Palmieri's hushed voice called in, "Jerry? Okay in there?"

"Yeah. Keep down. What'd you find out front?"

"I found a dead soldier, that's what. Half his head blown away. A marksman's medal was on the body."

Ciglia muttered a string of hushed profanities which was interrupted by another quiet report from the kitchen area. "Same back here, boss. Huck never knew what hit 'im. And one of those medals lying on his chest."

"Here, boss," the fourth man reported, stepping in quietly behind Palmieri. "I made a quick splice on that phone line. I don't know if it'll work or not."

"Try it! Get Del. Tell him I want his whole crew out here damn quck!"

"Sure, boss."

17

Ciglia had a quick change of mind. "Nate, you do it. Homer!"

"Yeah?"

"Where's the old man?"

"I left him upstairs."

"Oh hell, that's great, that's real wonderful. Probably choked on the smoke—or worse. Get up there and check 'im out. Careful, though. You don't know what's up there, eh."

There was no immediate response nor sound of movement from Homer Gallardo's general vicinity.

Ciglia growled, "Homer?"

"You, uh, want me to go up there and check 'im out, boss?"

"That's what I said!"

"Yessir. Uh—wonder maybe someone would like to back me up?"

"Let Homer play with the phones, Jerry," Palmieri suggested heavily. "I'll check the upstairs."

"I want you at *my* back!" Ciglia fumed. "What is this, all of a sudden, a goddamn caucus? Did I ask anybody for a vote? Homer, move your—*wait a minute*! Where's my woman? Nate! *Where's Toni*?"

"I didn't see her since the blast, Jerry."

"Well goddamn! God*damn*! I have to do everything my own self? You guys just jump out the damn windows and to hell with everything else?"

"It all happened so fast, Jerry," Palmieri apologized. "I figured you had her under your wing."

"You take Homer up there and shake this joint down!" Ciglia hissed furiously. "I mean wall to wall and floor by floor! Jake stays with me—this *goddamn* ankle! That bastard! I want his head, you hear me! I *want* that *boy*!"

"He's probably long gone," Palmieri whispered back from the stairway.

"So what the hell did he want here?" Ciglia growled.

18

"What did he want at Gulfport?" Gallardo commented, with obvious petulance. And it was the wrong thing to say, to the wrong man, at the wrong time.

Ciglia lashed out in the darkness at the sound of that sneering voice, catching the offender with an open-handed slap that sent him sprawling onto the shattered railing at the bottom of the stairs.

Steve Rocco's defeated tones rose from the darkness to fill the embarrassed silence that followed and to cap the events of the night. "Boss, I got to tell you this. It was Bolan, okay. He held a cannon to my head and made me yell while he tossed grenades. It was a setup. He didn't want anyone coming down those stairs. He wanted up there, boss. He wanted the upstairs to himself."

Palmieri's big feet were already pounding up the stairway. Lights went on up there as he rounded the curve and hurried on to the top level. Even Gallardo was galvanized into action, reaching the second floor just behind the chief bodyguard and racing into the master suite at full gallop.

All was silent below until Palmieri's quiet report floated down the stairwell. "The old man's gone, Jerry."

"So's your woman," Gallardo added breathlessly.

Ciglia growled, "Can you beat that. Now why do you suppose—"

"What the hell could Bolan want with that old man?" Jake Rio wondered aloud.

"Nothing good," Palmieri said testily as he descended the stairs.

Jerry Ciglia hobbled to a chair and dropped into it with a tired sigh. He said, "Somebody find me a cigarette. And let's have some lights on. The bastard's long gone from here now. He got what he wanted."

Gallardo brought a cigarette box and a lighter. Ciglia

19

thanked him, then told him, "Hey, Homer—I apologize, huh? I'm sorry I swatted you."

"It's okay, boss. I earned it."

"Go up and get me some clothes, huh?"

Gallardo grinned and hurried back upstairs.

Someone had found a functioning lamp in the shattered room and turned it on. Steve Rocco sat in a miserable heap on the couch, head in his hands. Everything looked much worse in the light.

"Well well," Ciglia mused.

Nate Palmieri locked gazes with him for a quiet moment, then said, "Guess I better make that call."

"Yeah," Ciglia said quietly. "We're going to get that old man back, Nate."

"I guess we better."

"I guess we damn well better." Ciglia sucked nervously on the cigarette and his eyes danced to some inner drummer as the full implications of that night in St. Louis descended upon him. "You got a good look at the guy, Stevie?" he asked quietly.

"Not really," Rocco replied in a muffled voice. "It was dark. I thought it was Huck, at first. He had this flashlight in my eyes. First I knew of trouble, this big cannon was in my face. Then the guy drops one of those medals . . . and that got to me, boss. I'm sorry but it just blew me out. He's standing there talking to me in this graveyard voice, looking holes through me. It was him, all right—everything I ever heard about the guy—and he had me shivered." Rocco swayed to his feet and staggered over to confront his boss head on. "I'm not trying to alibi it," he declared emotionally. "Just telling it like it was. That guy is—is . . ."

Ciglia's gaze dropped as he murmured, "I know, Steve—I know. Look—the day crew will be here pretty soon. Go on to bed. You look like hell." The big houseman gave Nate Palmieri a whipped look and slowly climbed the stairs.

Jake Rio was nervously pacing the floor just outside the blast zone. Ciglia sent him outside with instructions for the handling of the dead.

Palmieri was at the telephone. He showed his boss a conspiratorial smile and quietly announced, "It's noisy, but it's working. What do I tell them?"

"Tell them," Ciglia soberly instructed, "that our pigeon has come to us. Tell them I want a steel curtain around this town. Tell them I want to see blood running in the streets. Tell them it's open season on the old bunch—no exceptions—I want a clean sweep. Tell them—you know what to tell them, Nate."

Palmieri smiled coldly and spoke into the telephone. "Hello, Charlie. It's going down right now. The big one. Boss says Scramble Alert. You got any questions?"

He cradled the telephone and turned a smooth face to his boss. "Charlie had no questions."

"Okay, now try to get through to New York. Tell them the same thing you told Charlie."

"What if they ask about the old man?"

"Tell them that old man is dead and just waiting now for his burial. Tell them we're rounding up all his loyal subjects and inviting them to the services." He smiled hugely. "You know what to tell them about that old man, Nate."

"That old man" was, at that moment, resting in good hands on the back seat of Bolan's rented vehicle, his head pillowed on Toni Blancanales's lap.

"He's breathing good," the girl reported to the man up front.

"Conscious?"

"In and out. I believe he's stronger than he seems."

"Great," Bolan said. "I hope your maternal instincts are flowering because he's your new assignment. I want you to mother-hen him night and day. Get some nour-

21

ishment into him, but carefully. You can't risk a doctor or any outside help, so it's all up to you. Got me?"

"Got you," she replied. "Do you have a hideout in mind?"

"That's where we're headed."

"Have you seen the boys?" she inquired, referring to her partners.

"I have," he assured her. "They're okay."

She sighed. "I guess they're upset with me. I couldn't risk a contact. That guy Ciglia hasn't let me out of his sight since Monday night. Mack—wherever you're taking me, I'll need some clothes. I can't run around in this condition—not even in the company of a ninety-nine-year-old man."

He chuckled. "Especially not. We'll take care of that."

"Are you on our case now?"

"Not exactly. But I expect it'll work out to the same effect."

"I hope so," she said, pouting just a bit. "I was getting awfully close."

"It's all the same bag of worms, Toni. Touch one and it travels to them all. What were they hoping to get from Giamba?"

"I'm not sure. Whatever it is, they want it awfully bad. Jerry Ciglia is going to be very upset with you."

Bolan chuckled quietly at that.

He hoped Toni was correct. He wanted Ciglia upset enough to come out swinging with every punch he had. A dangerous game, sure, but the only game to play with an infestation such as this one. He had to bring them out of the woodwork everywhere, primed for a showdown and committed to an all-out war.

And that was *Bolan*'s game.

"This old man is pathetic," Toni commented dolefully. "I know—he's probably been as big a rat as any

22

of them, in his time, but this is awful, it's inhuman. He's skin and bones."

"This old man," Bolan told her, "is worse than a rat. He's a piranha, and he's stripped more bones than you've seen. He crawled from the same bag as those others, and don't for a minute forget that. He'd zap you with a switchblade from his deathbed, and don't forget *that*."

"This old man, he played one," Toni crooned softly, recalling the lyrics of a childhood song.

"One too many," Bolan told her.

Yeah. Give a dog a bone.

"This old man went rolling home." She sang it like a lullaby, unknowingly voicing the very thought that was in Bolan's mind.

Damn right.

That, too, was Bolan's game in St. Louis.

3: THE GUY

The Giamba empire had been under official police scrutiny for months, ever since Ciglia and his New York troops moved in on the territory. A special tactical intelligence unit headed by Lt. Tom Postum of SLPD had been given prime responsibility for maintaining cognizance of the shifting patterns of underworld power in the area, and Postum's unit was locked into a very tight cooperative liaison with an FBI task force established for the same purpose.

And the patterns had been shifting dramatically.

Several aged members of the Giamba Family had quietly "retired" and left the country. A few others had "gone over," accepting minor roles in the new crime organizaton being forged by newcomer Jerry Ciglia. Most, however, had simply dropped from view—either out of loyalty to Giamba or distrust of Ciglia—and appeared to be awaiting some word or sign from Giamba himself, who was also mysteriously submerged.

Little credence had been given to rumors of

Giamba's voluntary exile to Latin America. Such a move could be checked out and verified; there was no evidence to support the rumors. It was also generally believed in police circles that old man Giamba was still alive and "lying low" somewhere in the St. Louis area. The situation therefore seemed dangerously unstable and highly explosive. Some official worriers were predicting an imminent and unavoidable street war and, indeed, informant rumors of a Ciglia purge of Giamba loyalists had been growing day by day.

The Giamba mansion had been under direct surveillance for weeks, as were several other known centers of mob activity in the area. Telephone wiretaps had been authorized and instituted, and what small intelligence could be gleaned from the enigmatic mutterings harvested from that source only served to deepen official fears of a full-scale shootout between the dissident underworld factions.

Tom Postum was prepared for the worst, then, after being roused from his bed in the early morning hours with the report of an "apparent bombing" in the Giamba residence. He immediately relayed that information to his superior at Tactical Command, then hurriedly dressed and lost no time getting to headquarters for a full assessment of developments there.

Postum calculated a spread of less than twenty minutes from receipt of the call in his bed to the moment he walked through the door at Tac Command. Yet his watch commander was waiting for him with phone in hand and baffled curiosity on his face.

"Guy on here says he's Mack Bolan," the sergeant reported. "Asked for you by name. Says he has important information for you."

Postum frowned as he replied to that, "No time for games, Willis. I want to set up a—"

"Better take the call, Lieutenant. Whoever this guy is, he seems to know all about the blast at Giamba's."

Postum snatched the phone and spoke sharply into it. "What's the game here?"

A voice of quiet authority replied, "It's no game, Postum. I want you to know that I have Little Artie under my wing. He's alive and safe—for the moment, anyway. Now Ciglia, unless I've misread the guy completely, will be moving quickly to cut losses and consolidate his position. He—"

"Just a damn minute!" the cop snarled. "I believe you *are* Mack Bolan!"

"That's what I've always been told," that voice quietly replied. "Do you want to hear this or don't you?"

Postum gave the watch commander a confirming nod of the head and an eye signal, then resumed the conversation while the other cop scrambled over to the intercept system.

"How long have you been in our town, Gangbuster?" he asked casually.

"Long enough to know the size of the problem," was the cool reply. "Ciglia is in full charge here, now—working a franchise directly from New York. He's going to turn your town and your state into a mob playground like there's never been before, or so he believes. He just might pull it off, too, if he can get past the problem of one frail old man."

"Giamba, of course."

"Right. Ciglia has been trying to finesse through a smooth transfer of power to save local fireworks but Artie wouldn't play that game, not even under starvation and other subtle tortures. Finesse really isn't Ciglia's normal game. I believe he's been acting under restraints from the New York head shed. Now that I have Giamba, those restraints mean nothing. Ciglia has probably already written the old man off as dead. I'm expecting him to be moving very quickly now along the other path."

Postum could hardly believe the audacity of the

bastard. "Do you know what you've done, dude?" he asked disgustedly.

"Sure," that strong voice replied. "I've killed the hopes for a smooth transfer of power. I read that as a plus, not a minus."

"What's this plus-minus bullshit?" Postum spat bitterly. "I'm talking about blood in the streets, man! You've thrown the town into a gang war, that's what you've done!"

"Which simply means that the town has a fighting chance," the cool bastard replied. "Isn't that better than total defeat? How would you like to be carrying your morning reports to a mob torpedo for the rest of your life, Postum?"

The lieutenant from Tac Intelligence simply could not believe this guy! He sputtered, "I'm not debating the ethics of—with a . . . what the hell is this, mister? You've got a hell of a goddamned nerve calling me up like this and . . ."

The guy at the other end of that tense line was chuckling quietly at Postum's rage. The cop shut himself off abruptly and flashed a sheepish grin at the watch commander.

"You're something else—do you know that?" he said calmly to the most wanted man in America. "Are you the one bombed the Giamba place awhile ago?"

"I am. It was just a couple of flash grenades, but it got what I wanted."

"Uh huh. What else do you want, Bolan?"

"Twenty-four hours."

"What's that supposed to mean? Twenty-four hours of what?"

"Police cooperation."

"There you go again! You're a *loony*, guy!"

"Maybe so," the guy said, sighing a bit sadly. "But I keep on hoping. Look, Postum, I called you because I've been assured that you're an intelligent cop. And

28

you *are* in the tactical game so why not *think* tactics? Let the war rage. Look the other way, and give it twenty-four hours. The enemy will engage itself and I'll be in there helping both sides exterminate the other. This time tomorrow I'll be out of your town, and what's left of the local mob and their corrupted politicians won't be worth the expense of jailing."

"That's crazy and you know it. I can't sell a—"

"I know you can't." The guy chuckled again. It sounded like ice clinking into a deep glass. "That's the major difference, I guess, between a cop and a soldier. I *am* a soldier, Postum. And I *have* to think tactics. Actually, I called to tell you that the war is definitely on, and to suggest that you get your quiet cops to safety."

"What quiet cops?"

"Your intelligence unit has, at my count, a minimum of six undercover men working the—"

"Okay, okay!" Postum interrupted quickly. It made him nervous to hear even departmental officials discussing his undercover operations. Here *this* guy was. . . . "Now let me tell you something, Bolan. I appreciate your concern for the safety of police officers but it doesn't buy you a damn thing. We're not looking the other way here, mister, and we don't need your kind of help to solve our problems. What's more, if I—"

"Sorry," the guy cut in. "My time is up. Good talking to you, Postum. Stay hard."

The line clicked dead and the Tac lieutenant turned his irritation to the watch commander.

"Not enough time," the sergeant reported, shaking his head. "It came through a north side exchange. That's as far as we got."

"That damn guy," Postum said wonderingly. "Did you *hear* that damn guy?"

The watch commander was smiling soberly. "Too

29

bad, isn't it? Sounds like an okay guy. Tragic. Very tragic."

"Save that shit for his funeral service," the lieutenant savagely commented. "But don't bother to write it down—there won't be time enough to forget it."

"Mack Bolan," the sergeant went on, his tone unaltered, "in St. Louis. Can you beat that? I never suspected the guy would turn up here."

"Don't make it sound like such an honor," Postum growled. He was moving toward his office as he spoke. "Pull that tape and make sure you got a good print. Then call the captain and tell him I want to bring it in for his evaluation."

"Oh—I meant to tell you. He's called a meeting of unit heads, his office, in . . ." the sergeant glanced at the clock, ". . . five minutes."

"Check that tape," Postum called back. "I'll take it with me."

He went into his office and closed the door, then sat on the edge of his desk, pulled a knee up and clasped it in both hands, and allowed the pent grin to break across his usually sober face.

"That damn guy," he murmured admiringly.

4:   THIS OLD WORLD

Toni had come out of that smoking house wearing nothing but bikini briefs, weight about one ounce and covering power practically zero. Luckily, Bolan was carrying a change of clothes for himself in the rented car—slacks and shirt—which he promptly made available to the girl.

She turned up her nose at the ridiculously overlarge slacks but demurely slipped into the shirt, which covered her petite figure like a shortie nightgown and merely accentuated the natural appeal of the equipment it covered.

She moved into the front seat while Bolan made his call to the law, satisfied that Artie Giamba was in no immediate danger of dying.

When Bolan returned and they were rolling again, she sniffed, "Sorry I'm so hard to look at in my nothings."

She knew better than that.

"That's not the situation," Bolan replied soberly. "I

have enough problems without driving around town with a naked lady in my car."

She laughed softly and lay her head against his shoulder. "I know. I was just fishing for a compliment. It's okay, Mack. I can take it if you want to tell me that the mere sight of my exposed flesh fills you with shrieking desire. It won't cost you a thing, either."

He grinned, remembering another time. "It cost me damn near a week, once," he reminded her.

She pressed against him and sighed. "Yeah. If that's what you call living large, Sergeant Bolan, then it's been nothing but *small* for me ever since. Mack ... I've missed you terribly. And I'll bet you'd forgotten I'm alive. Hadn't you?"

"Still fishing?"

She said, "Sure. It's okay. I can take it if you want to tell me your life has been nothing but tears and despair ever since we've been apart. I won't believe it, anyway, and we can both enjoy the thrill of the lie."

He told her, "Toni, you're very special."

"To you?"

"Sure."

"Do you still have that beautiful mobile honeymoon suite?"

She was referring to the warwagon, in which she and Bolan had traveled west from the New Orleans war zone—several tough lifetimes ago.

"I have it," he assured her.

"It's okay to tell me you love me. It won't cost—"

Bolan simply had to put a stop to that. He cut her off with a sharp rebuke. "Toni! What's eating you?"

She wriggled away from him and replied, "Nothing."

"If it's Ciglia, don't let it."

"I feel so damn dirty," she sniffed.

"So okay, we're both dirty," he said harshly. "You bed them, I bleed them. You don't mention the blood on me, I don't mention the paw marks on you. Play

32

your high school parlor games with the kids back home, Toni."

"You just go straight to hell!" she flared back.

He muttered, "I'm already there."

She flung herself back upon him, wrapping his free arm in both of hers. "I'm sorry," she softly apologized. "I didn't mean that."

"It's okay," he replied, just as softly. "I understand it, Toni. Used to fight the same devils in myself. Still do, now and then. Look, kid—it's that kind of world. *This* world, I mean. The one you and I have joined. We can't function here with the values of that other world. Nice guys and good girls just don't contribute anything here—and, dammit, you can't live in both worlds. You can't play the games in this one under the rules designed for that other one."

"Let's see," she murmured, "you're saying that you don't judge me the same way you would if we were just a guy and a girl trying to get it on, back home. You don't despise me for—for . . ."

He sighed. These were the hard moments. "If I judge you at all, Toni, it's through your professional abilities—your effectiveness in *this* world. And I don't despise anybody."

She shook her head at that. "You despise that old man back there."

"Uh uh. I understand him. I recognize his threat to that other world. I'll take whatever steps I consider necessary to neutralize that effect. But I don't hate that old man, Toni. In certain ways, I even admire him."

She had her knees beneath her, now, perched sidewise on the seat and peering unblinkingly into his profile.

"I guess I'm still getting to know you," she whispered.

"Look at the blood on me, then," he quietly suggested. "And ask yourself how far simple hatred can

33

propel a man through Blood River. Hate doesn't move me, Toni. Once, maybe, it could and did. No more. I've lost the capacity for hate."

"What moves you then, Mack Bolan?"

"You writing a thesis?"

"Maybe."

He flicked a sharp glance her way and replied, "This old world moves me, Toni."

"You mean this *new* world, not the old one."

He nodded. "This one is where the battles are fought. But it's not new. To you and me, sure, it's new. It has always been here, though—maybe longer than the other one."

"I'm getting confused," she told him. "What's the name of this world of ours? *This* one."

"Hell," he said softly.

"What?"

"This is hell, Toni."

She whispered, "Oh wow. I think I'm beginning to . . ."

They drove on, through a moment of rather pregnant silence. Toni was gazing through the side glass, apparently trying to orient herself to the countryside. Dawn was breaking.

Presently she sighed and said, "You're blowing me out, you know. Why didn't we ever talk like this before?"

"It just never came up, I guess," he replied.

"This is really Hell, huh?"

"As a state of mind, sure. This is where that other world—that safe world—is made, shaped, motivated. It all comes from right here. This is where the soldiers are. It's a place where armies clash in the night—constantly, endlessly, eternally."

"Does that make me a soldier?" she asked soberly.

"Sure does. They come in all shapes, sizes, and sexes. And in two polarities—two sides—two only."

"The good and the bad," Toni decided.

He shrugged. "Or the right and the wrong, call it how you please. In that other world, see, the whole thing is done in shades of gray. In this one, it's either light or darkness."

"And you weren't just being poetic. You really believe all that. The world of good girls and nice guys is simply a spin-off, a by-product of this one."

"Haven't you ever wondered," he replied quietly, "about the price tag for a civilization like that one—where girls can be always good and guys always nice? That's an Eden world, Toni, and it was hacked from a wilderness. Have you ever been in a jungle? You can hack a trail three feet wide in the morning and, by nightfall, that trail has disappeared, the jungle has reclaimed its own. Who do you think built Eden—and who is keeping it there? Good girls? Nice guys?" He shook his head. "Those are the children of the garden. Wouldn't know which side of the machete to hack with. Eden is built *out here,* Toni, in the jungle. The garden is a projection from hell."

She shivered, then leaned against him, both arms snaking across his shoulders in a tight embrace. "I don't like it out here, Mack," she said in a small voice.

"Neither do I," he told her. "There's still time for you, Toni. You can get out."

"But you can't?"

"You know I can't. Look at the blood on me—just look at it."

She began to cry and he pushed her away, his jaw clamping and the eyes settling once again into icy depths. "Don't do that to me," he said.

"I don't like this damn world of yours, Mack Bolan!" she declared emotionally.

"I didn't build it," he replied. "I just live here. Those who live here, die here. If you've got other plans, then I can probably stop this world long enough for you to get off. But don't drop sad tears on me, Toni. They're infectious. And if I ever start, I'd drown this whole damn world with mine."

"*You*?" she gasped unbelievingly. "*Cry*?"

"Not if I can help it," he said harshly.

He pulled the car to the side of the road and turned to the girl with a penetrating gaze. "We don't live here by accident, Toni. It's by decision, and 100 percent commitment. It's time for you to decide."

He thrust a small wallet into her hands.

"There's money in your hands and a motel one block over. Make your move."

She threw the wallet at him and settled herself sedately in the seat. "No way," she said quietly, speaking through slackening tears. "Consider me properly chastised and let's go on with the show."

"You're sure," he pressed her.

"Sure I'm sure. Give me my damn machete and let's go hack some trails."

Bolan grinned soberly as he eased the car back onto the road. She was his kind of woman. And that was bad. Mack Bolan's inner reservoir of dammed tears could attest to the badness of that.

His kind usually died young, in this old world.

5: SOMEWHERE

A reconstituted Able Team was together, functional, and once again pounding along the hellfire trails—and Mack Bolan had to admit in his heart that he felt better with the reinforcements.

In Vietnam, they had been the penetration team to draw the dirtier missions, the more impossible details. "Able Team can do it" had been the quiet battle cry of that day—and Mack Bolan was not the only reason for that record of excellence.

Gadgets Schwarz was the sort of guy who would lie for days on end in a clump of growth at the edge of a VC village, gathering electronic intelligence with a barrel audio pickup—totally unsupported, isolated by miles from every friendly hand, subsisting on hard crumbs and damn little water—then return to base camp with dry-wit tales of VC sentries pissing on his legs in broad daylight and bringing their women to bed in the weeds beside him at night, ". . . just one crazy hard-on away from where I'm lying."

37

Blancanales had earned his nickname, Politician, during an earlier era while with the Special Forces in the pacification program. When he came to the penetration teams, some began calling him "the chameleon" in tribute to his ability to become practically invisible in most any environment. It was not a matter of costume camouflage, either. The guy had the knack of simply blending with any background or gathering. He had once walked undetected with a small group of native fieldhands the entire length of an enemy-held village— *in full field-combat garb*—purchased food at the local market, and again casually strolled out the way he'd come.

Bolan had learned much from each of these men— both in Vietnam and later when he'd formed his Death Squad of Mafia fighters in Los Angeles. The LA venture had quickly proven to be a tragic mistake. Of the ten men comprising that squad, only Bolan, Schwarz, and Blancanales survived the Los Angeles war with the DiGeorge Family. Bolan had walked his trails more or less alone ever since, except for a brief job in San Diego with these two old partners.

During the New Orleans campaign, he'd stumbled onto them purely by chance—and luckily so, for them. There was barely a spark of life left between the two of them when Bolan rescued the pair from the torture-interrogation activities of Tommy Carlotti, the self-styled terror of Bourbon Street. As here in St. Louis, they'd been doing an investigative job for a client, and the "client" turned out to be . . .

Bolan sighed and turned his mind from that. He could not and would not presume to live these men's lives for them. If they wanted into his world again, for a while, then they were welcome. But, let the devil claim his own. Bolan could not afford the weight of another broken friend upon his soul—he would accept no moral responsibility for what might become of them in his world.

It was their world, too, the moment they knocked on the door and walked inside. The nineteenth-century poet and dramatist, Henrik Ibsen, had once written: "The strongest man in the world is he who stands most alone." Bolan himself expanded that idea when he jotted it into his journal with the parenthetical note: "Every man who stands, stands alone."

And a few hours earlier, he had given voice to the idea as he solemnly told his temporary partners: "It's damn good to be together again. Just remember, though—in this world, togetherness is an illusion. Not one of us can bleed for the other. Every man has to do his own dying. And his own living. So let's not allow the illusion to defeat us. We stand stronger when we stand alone . . . and know it."

Schwarz's response to that had been: "Sure, Sarge. I learned that years ago. It's like making love."

Blancanales scowled at the electronics genius and asked him, "What the hell does what he said have to do with making love?"

"Nobody can do it for you," Schwarz solemnly explained.

The Politician threw up his hands and told Bolan: "He's relating it to the only thing he really understands. I've never seen such a cocksman. I never realized—listen, this is God's truth—this guy has five or six women in every town we hit. Right here in St. Louis, already, he has—"

"They're contacts," Schwarz said quickly, his face flaming. "Don't make it sound like—"

"Contacts, my ass!" Blancanales howled. "How come you make all your contacts lying down, Gadgets?"

It was characteristic of those two to turn a sober subject into something to chuckle over—while at the same time conveying an understanding and acceptance of the business at hand. And Bolan was grinning now in the remembrance of that pleasant banter. It was the part of that other world he missed most—the comradeship, the happy brushing with other minds and other personalities in relaxed friendship.

He had gone on, then, to check the guys out on the warwagon's special systems, then turned it over for their use during the coming hours of intrigue and bloodshed.

Both had been highly impressed with the $100,000 marvel of space-age engineering—Gadgets Schwarz, in particular.

A NASA scientist, working with another genius from a New Orleans-based electronics firm, had moonlighted the sophisticated electronics systems for Bolan, giving him access to the very latest technological wonders of the day. Others had contributed their own specialties and equipment to produce the finished result: a battle cruiser which served as a mobile base camp, command post, field headquarters, armory, spy ship—all packed into twenty-six feet of solid luxury and comfort.

GMC supplied the stock features—the basic body, a slightly modified 455-cubic-inch Toronado engine, automatic transmission with front traction, rear tandem wheels with air-bag suspension—a galley, shower and toilet, bunk space.

Bolan had added one-way glass throughout, allowing 360-degree visibility for himself while shielding the interior from curious eyes. Amidships was a foldaway light-table for running combat plots, a central command console whose functions could be remoted to the control deck forward, a weapons lab and armory with concealed storage for munitions and weapons.

The features that inspired Schwarz to near ecstasy involved the electronic intelligence-gathering gear. The heart of that system was computerized selection and switching circuits which controlled radio pickups,

40

highly sensitive audio scanners, optic selections, plus a special console for synchronizing, time-phasing, sorting, editing, re-recording and storing collected intelligence data.

Pol's heart had immediately gone to the weapons lab and the cruiser's heavy punch capability: the swivel-platform, retractable rocket pod concealed in the roof. The system was operated from the driver's console by highly sophisticated fire-control gear featuring night-bright optics and automatic target acquisition. Upon command, the launcher would rise through sliding panels to the roof, lock into firing position, "acquire" target, and deliver massive destruction over an impressive range.

The guys had happily taken charge of Bolan's battle cruiser and they'd been out cruising the territory most of the night, consolidating their own intelligence posture and, hopefully, adding to it a few significant items specifically requested by Bolan.

The operation in St. Louis was going to demand some damned tight numbers, unfailing timing, and an incredible degree of "finesse."

Bolan had still not completely discounted the earlier misgivings concerning the possibility that Ciglia and the entire mob movements in this area were little more than an elaborately baited trap for Bolan himself. Certainly the old men in New York had grown querulously weary of "the Bolan problem." They had already spent fortunes and moved mountains to end the problem. Bolan's direct line to *La Commissione*, Leo Turrin, had sent repeated warnings of supersecret strategy sessions and concerted movements, all directed toward the demise of the man who was shaking their house with ever-increasing ferocity.

It could not go on forever; Bolan realized that. Sooner or later he was bound to make a fatal slip, or the fates would turn their smiles elsewhere, and the brief "problem" of Mack Bolan would abruptly go where all other Mafia problems seemed to go: into nowhere.

But, what the hell, he'd never expected to live forever. He had not expected, in fact, to live this long. That "last mile" which began in Pittsfield—hell, how many eternities ago?—had now spanned the world and seemed to be extending into infinity—but he knew that this also was an illusion.

The "last mile" could not be measured in distance traveled but in blood spilled. How much more could he spill before his own was spent into the final pool? Not much, probably. He was tired, battle weary, soul sensitive. It was why he'd unloaded on Toni that way. It was why he'd gone so somber with Blancanales and Schwarz. The end was near: Bolan could feel it in his bones.

Would this be the final campaign?

He shook his head at that.

Only God could say. And God was a neutral. He created the heavens and the earth, okay. Then he created man, and commanded him to give some meaning to existence.

So men built a hell—and, from that, fought and scratched to construct a paradise.

And for why?

Bolan had no answers for that.

If there was a God, somewhere—a thinking, rational God, with a mind bigger and better than Bolan's—then surely he saw the whole production with at least the same detachment and understanding as Bolan.

A God who deserved the name wouldn't despise an old man like Artie Giamba. He might even admire certain things about him.

Was God a neutral?

If a *man* could *care*—why couldn't God?

It mattered, sure. Somewhere the universe wept over

42

each loss and rejoiced with every gain. The whole bloody, savage business mattered—somewhere.

It mattered to Mack Bolan. And he was somewhere. For a while, anyway. As long as he lived, then, it mattered somewhere whether there would be light or darkness upon the earth. That was reason enough right there for Mack Bolan.

Reason enough to go on living—to go on killing—to keep on wading Blood River.

He'd seen Toni and Giamba safely tucked away. His scouts were out taking a final reading of the situation. The sun was edging into the eastern sky. The die was cast. Ready or not, the time was here and the showdown was near.

For awhile, anyway, old Saint Louie was going to shake, rattle and roll. And then—somewhere—the universe would weep or rejoice.

And yes, Toni, there were devils inside Mack Bolan from time to time. He could not have said, at that moment, just which side he thought the universe may be pulling for.

6:   EVERYWHERE

Bolan dropped off his rental car and made the switch to the "Saint Louie Junker"—a five-year-old sedan whose dented body and flaking paint concealed a powerful and finely tuned warhorse for the coming activities. A supply of personal weapons and ammo lay beneath a blanket on the rear floor, the trunk was crammed with munitions, and the vehicle was radio-equipped.

The time was seven o'clock, Saturday morning. The town was quiet—hushed, even—with very little vehicular traffic, stores closed. It was that eerie hour for big cities.

He pointed the car toward Busch Stadium and punched in the pre-set combat channel on the radio.

"North Star," he called. "What's the lay?"

Schwarz's soft tones bounced back immediately. "Snap in Charlie Sector."

Bolan selected a glass slide from a dash-mounted case and dropped it into a miniature projector which occupied the seat beside him. The slide was a duplicate

45

of one from the warwagon's console plot. A street map, in sharp detail, covering the city's riverfront, leapt onto a small screen mounted beneath the dashboard.

"Charlie it is," he reported to the mother ship.

"We're at coordinates Delta Five, cruising north, speed thirty."

Bolan's gaze flicked to the map display. They were headed up Broadway, from a point just north of Eads Bridge.

"Roger," he replied. "Tracking from Easy Four." He swung immediately onto Grand Boulevard and powered northward for an intercept route. "Situation report."

"Situation is grooving," Schwarz told him. "Caravan sprung from Stonehenge at zero six forty. Estimate twenty units in three big blacks. Probable destination, Winevat. Instructions."

Interpreted, the report meant that three crew wagons carrying about twenty guns were running from Del Annunzio's fortress in Webster Groves on an apparent headhunting mission and seemed to be headed toward the secret hideout of Jules Pattriccia, oldest and dearest friend of Little Artie Giamba. Pattriccia had made his first stake during prohibition days, running juice from a little winery in the Missouri Ozarks, and still carried the tag "Vino Jules." Annunzio was a frontline gunnery lieutenant under Jerry Ciglia, sharing top honors in that department wth one Charlie Alimonte.

Bolan's instructions to the warwagon were: "Maintain quiet running until endtrack verified. Report developments."

"Roj."

"No more flights?"

"Affirm. Flights everywhere, but most are soft runs. Electronic verified. This one is hard. Also, unusual official activity."

"Roj, North Star. Maintain."

46

"Maintaining."

Blancanales and Schwarz had "wired" the town long before Bolan's arrival on the scene—which simply meant that they had located and identified most of the Mafia elements present and had them under electronic surveillance. The special collection gear aboard the warwagon fitted beautifully into that surveillance network, allowing the guys to harvest more intelligence data in an hour than they could have covered all day without it.

Schwarz's closing report to Bolan reflected the value of that capability. They knew that various head parties were on the prowl but that only Annunzio appeared to have a specific target in mind. Therefore, the Bolan forces could zero in on the paydirt and forget, for the moment, the fishing expeditions.

Also, thanks to the warwagon's radio scanners, all police frequencies were under constant monitor and provided a rather reliable gauge of "official activity."

As for the principals, Bolan had the full story on old Jules Pattriccia and his riverfront diggings out past Merchants Bridge. The one he was vague on was Annunzio.

"Give me a read on that caravan leader," he requested from Schwarz. "Look in File Three."

"Roj. Stand by."

Bolan swung onto upper Broadway and continued the chase at a leisurely pace while Schwarz consulted the warwagon's personnel bank.

The search took about ten seconds.

Schwarz reported, "Age twenty-eight. First Family favorite son, once removed. Six taps in Hardtown through last October, none binding. Present connections via Iron Mike. He's a soft tiger."

Sparse though it was, the rundown refreshed Bolan's memory. The file simply reported that Annunzio was the son of a once-powerful underboss in the Manhattan family of Augie Marinello, that he'd had six felony arrests and no convictions, that his last known job before joining Ciglia was as a *commissione* gunner under Mike Talifero, and that he was educated and polished but mean as a snake.

And, yeah, Bolan knew more than that about that dude.

"Use caution," he warned his forward trackers. "He's a slicker."

"Understand," Schwarz replied.

"I am now running true. Acquire and report."

"Roger," was the immediate response. "Have you at Delta Nine and tracking true. Range, one thousand meters."

Bolan was working the backtrack now, deliberately falling behind to scout the rear. "Now falling away to backboard," he advised the mother ship. He ejected the Charlie Sector slide and dropped in another. "Will attempt a rejoin at Bravo Two Delta. Close your track all possible and advise immediately any deviation to base track. It's a Code Zebra."

"Roger, understand," Schwarz replied.

"Zebra" was an attack code, a Bolan classic when working with allies, tried and proven in the hardgrounds of Southeast Asia and just as appropriate here as anywhere. And, yes, Schwarz would certainly "understand."

Del Annunzio was a "soft tiger," all right.

Bolan was taking no chances whatever with that guy.

The squawk line from the communications center carried the report to Lt. Postum: "There's a couple of weird mobile radios running around out there. I've heard every kind of CB-band roadcode there is, and this is nothing like that."

Postum looked up from his planning sheet and fixed

48

the intercom with an interested gaze. "What do you make it?"

"I don't make it, that's the problem. Sounds sort of like military, but it's the wrong band for that. I thought at first it might be a couple of boats on the river, but they're moving too fast for boats. I'm getting a good plot, now, and it's definitely overland. Too slow for aircraft except helicopters, and there's no mistaking a helicopter carrier."

The lieutenant surged to his feet as he called back, "I'm coming in for a listen."

He reached the comm center just in time to overhear another of the "weird" exchanges.

"North Star, we've got a bandit back here. Mark him at one hundred meters off my head. Acquire and verify."

Postum's hackles went to full rise. That voice . . .

"See?" the technician was commenting. "Sounds like military aircraft, doesn't it. But it's not. I even considered a National Guard exercise, but that's out, too."

"Affirm, Backboard, I have acquisition, true and running one hundred meters off your head."

The technician was frowning. "It's a mixed jargon. Truckers talk that way sometimes, passing warnings on speed traps and such, but I—"

"It's not truckers," Postum said sourly.

"Give me a separation count," that damned voice commanded.

"Separation is one two zero zero meters, Backboard."

"Good enough. I am clearing the backtrack."

"Tally ho, Backboard."

"Commencing run. Backboard out."

The technician grinned. "Sounds like a torpedo attack on the *Goldenrod*, doesn't it?"

"Let's see your ADF plot," Postum quietly ordered.

An automated wall display came alive with com-

49

puterized light sequences superimposed on a grid map of the metro area. "River route, north," the tech needlessly pointed out.

Postum growled, "Yeah. Okay. Something's definitely going down. Route a replay of that to the lab. I want a voiceprint comparison with the telephone tape I sent in awhile ago. I want it quick."

The technician was busy at his console. "Pretty cagey guys, whoever they are. Tight radio discipline. Had a hell of a time lining in the ADFs. Very brief transmissions—and I couldn't make a damn thing of their lingo. Could you?"

"Enough," Postum replied grimly. He was eyeing the grid map as he spoke. "Buzz the skipper. Tell him we're recommending a Tac Alert in Sector Four. Tell him I'm bringing in the hard intelligence for command evaluation."

The intelligence boss spun on his heel and hurried off to the electronics lab.

He could not understand himself. He should be feeling elated, triumphant—at the very least, self-satisfied.

But he felt none of that.

That damned guy—that damned, superlative guy. *We're sending the armored hounds after you, guy!*

But there was nothing at all for sober Tom Postum to grin about, now.

7: ATTACK ZONE

They were on grim and serious business, and it was a grimly silent bunch who were packed into the big crew wagon.

George "Hooker" Napoli was sprawled comfortably across the front seat, sharing it only with Spider Fischetti, the wheelman. The other five of the gun crew were squeezed into the rear area—shotgunners Rossi and Monaco wedged into the jump seats with their sawed-off weapons between their legs—pistolmen Verducco, Avante, and DiCavalla sharing the far rear seat.

These were not your typical Mafia street soldiers whose primary designs on life were as illegal entrepreneurs—"business" men who lived by their own rules and used force only as an adjunct to their money-making activities. These "boys" were professional guns. The guns they lived by *were* their business and their only claim to usefulness to an organization which existed for the sole purpose of acquiring riches.

"It's about time we started using station wagons,"

someone groused from the rear, with a sigh of discomfort.

The wheelman glanced into the rearview mirror for eye contact with the speaker. "That's when I quit," he declared calmly.

"They don't make Cadillac station wagons," explained another disgruntled voice from the rear. "Spider wouldn't get caught dead in anything so low class."

"That's not it," the wheelman protested amiably. "Class is not something you wear outside, especially. Not in a car, anyway. See, they—"

"It's easy to feel classy when you got a whole seat to yourself," said the first complainer. "Wonder how he'd like it with his knees jammed into his chest."

"Knock it off," Napoli growled.

"Sorry, Hooker," the wheelman apologized from the side of his mouth.

"Chit chat makes me nervous," the crew chief said. "You want to talk, okay, you got something you don't understand about the job, okay, but none of this jawing back and forth."

"Sure, Hooker."

Monaco, a new recruit, leaned forward from the jump seat and said, "It makes me nervous, too, Hooker. I don't like cruising around in broad daylight with all this hardware. We go through a stoplight, even, and we're in deep shit right away."

Napoli nodded his head and replied, "Okay, that's a legitimate worry. And it's job-connected. You want to talk about it?"

"I just did, Hooker. That's all I got to say."

The crew chief grunted and cleared his throat. "This is your first hit, that's why. Tell 'im, Spider, what we do in a case like that."

"We don't accept no damn tickets," the wheelman explained with a glance into the mirror.

52

Napoli growled, "What d'you think all this damn hardware is *for?*"

Someone sneered from the rear, "Dead traffic cops don't write tickets."

Monaco relaxed against his backrest and stroked the stock of his shotgun. "Okay. Now I know."

"You'd get the honors," the crew chief said, with a sober wink at Monaco. "You and your partner there. *Boom ba-boom.* No deep shit at all, see."

The shotgunner grinned sourly and glanced at the man beside him.

"How would you like that?" Napoli prodded, ignoring his own injunction against "jawing."

"What? Take out a cop?" Monaco shrugged. "Makes no difference to me. A head is a head."

Napoli was grinning hugely. "I knew I had me a boy," he said proudly. "You other boys hear that? A head is a head. This boy just got himself a name. From now on, you call him *Heads.*"

Spider Fischetti chuckled at that. "Know what we call a *head* in the navy?"

The newly christened shotgunner muttered, "You better cut that shit out, Spider."

The wheelman hastily apologized. It was a serious breach of etiquette in this curious world to make jokes about a "made" name.

Perhaps to change the subject, as much as for any other reason, Fischetti became very busy at his rearview mirror. "That, uh, old clunker back there, Hooker. About a block back? See 'im? Been hanging in there awhile now. You notice?"

"We passed him back there a ways," Napoli replied, flicking an unconcerned glance through the back window.

"Yeah, we did. But he's pacing us now."

One of the rear men said, "I been checking him. Keeps pulling up and falling back. Nervous driver.

53

Lots of guys do that. We can't all be wheelmen like Spider."

Fischetti chuckled at that. A moment later, he asked his boss, "Want me to fake 'im out, Hooker?"

"Forget it," Napoli replied. "Can't get paranoid about every damn car on the road. We're not here to worry about *our* tails."

"What *are* we doing way back here?" Monaco grumbled. "It'll all be over by the time we get there."

"You got an *itchy* boy there," Fischetti commented to the crew chief.

Napoli said, "That's the idea, Heads. We're like the second wave. With a guy like Bolan around, you can't be too careful. Don't worry, Del knows what he's doing."

Fischetti asked, "You think Bolan might really horn in up there?"

"I can't think of any reason why he should," Napoli replied. "But Dell says we make a sandwich, so dammit we make a sandwich."

"That's the guy gives me the shivers," said a pistoleer from the far back. "That Bolan, I mean. You think he's here on serious business, Hooker?"

"Who knows?" the crew chief replied with a shrug. "We can only take 'em one at a time. Right? Right now we're taking Vino Jules. We'll worry about Bolan when his turn comes."

The mention of Bolan seemed to have had a dampening effect on the occupants of that vehicle. The grim atmosphere of edgy silence settled in once again.

Presently, one of the men in the rear quietly offered, "He's just one guy. You know how these reputations get blown up. Like Heads said . . . a head is a head."

"Not that one, though," Fischetti commented soberly. "It's worth a million greens."

"I'll take a piece of that," Monaco growled.

Napoli and Fischetti exchanged knowing glances.

"Yeah, I think I got me a boy," the crew chief declared.

Bolan had the sandwich car "made" and he was pacing it into an appropriate attack zone. He wanted to make his run in an open area, preferably along a straightaway where he could be assured of a proper "safe zone" free of complicating factors and devoid of uninvolved bystanders. He had to confine his war to the proper places. He could not subject innocent people to the dangers of open warfare.

And he found his place some little distance north of the Merchants Bridge approach, in an industrial zone where the city seemed to have not yet awakened to the new day.

He had made good use of the intervening time, assuring himself via the warwagon's tracking systems that there was adequate separation between the two halves of the "sandwich" so that the sounds of warfare in the one sector would not alert those in the other.

And now, all conditions having been met, he was ready to make his move. He sent the "junker" surging ahead as he touched the mike button to advise his own troops, "Commencing run. Backboard out."

The target vehicle was moving sedately along, remaining well below the posted speed limit. Bolan's hot heap closed the gap without effort, and he was swinging around them in the pass before that sullen bunch in there awakened to the maneuver.

The wheelman was the first to notice, evidently catching the reflected motion in his side-mounted mirror—and Bolan saw the guy stiffen and yell something.

His front bumper was even with their rear when he let off on the gas and pumped the brake pedal to ease alongside, fully abreast now, pacing them down the straightaway.

No other traffic was in view, front or rear.

55

Both sides of the road were clear of structures.

This was *nowhere*.

The wheelman in the target car was tossing Bolan quick, angry glances and guys were moving around over there.

Bolan saw the snout of a tommy gun coming up off the front floorboards on the far side.

The rear window on the inside began smoothly lowering under powered control, the gaping twin muzzle of a sawed-off double-barrel riding the glass down—and this was precisely what Bolan had been awaiting.

He backhanded a heavy HE grenade through that lowering gunport and immediately tromped his brakes, hard, the front end of his vehicle nosing down in the squealing breakaway—and he had but a glimpse of the sudden panic erupting in that crowded vehicle as the shotgun ba-loomed harmlessly into the pavement which he had occupied one heartbeat earlier.

Timing, yeah—that was the clincher in any life-or-death exercise, and Bolan had been crowding his to the outer limit.

He'd put a five-second fuse on that grenade, and he was still squealing and bucking around in their backwash when the thing blew.

The shattering blast, contained and intensified by those close quarters, filled the interior of that screeching vehicle with an expansive ball of flame, formed a concave bulge in the roof, sent both rear doors springing outward to disgorge smoking human forms—and, finally, as an aftereffect, sent the doomed crew wagon plunging off the road and settling on its side in flaming wreckage.

There could not have been much left alive in there but Bolan halted the Saint Louie Junker at a safe distance and climbed out with a chatter gun for the mop-up. It was not blood lust that sent the man out there but compassion. To kill quick and clean was one thing. To die slowly in shrieking agony quite another.

He sprayed the wreckage with a full clip of thirty-calibre steeljackets, dropped a medal on the ground beside it, and walked back to check the guys who'd been blasted clear.

The first one he reached was obviously dead, his face a pulp, clothing in flames.

The other was twisted around a shotgun—big guy, tough-looking, but hardly more than a kid.

And he was alive ... momentarily. Bolan could not figure out why. Half his chest was missing and the cavity was awash with bubbling blood; he could even see the heart pumping. One eye only was open, and that eye was watching Mack Bolan.

He said, "Sorry, kid," and extended the chattergun in a one-hand hold.

Somewhere the kid found a voice although it did not sound much like one—not a human one.

"A head ... is not ... a head. Give ... me ... chance."

"Chances are all used up, kid." Bolan pumped a short burst from the fresh clip into that head, hastening the inevitable process already set in motion.

He dropped a bull's-eye cross atop that tragedy and muttered, "It was a hard world, kid. You can go home now. Better luck next time out."

He returned quickly to the junker, stowed his weapon, and grabbed the radio mike.

"This is Backboard," he announced tiredly. "I'm coming in."

"Just in time," was the immediate response. "We are engaged."

8:   GOING DOWN

What was it Bolan had said? Something about the difference between *cops* and *soldiers*?

Well—what the hell?

These men were not cops—certainly not command cops—and these were not police methods being discussed here. These guys, dammit, were *soldiers*—and what was happening here could only be described as a *combat briefing*.

Throw the damned stereotypes away and forget everything you ever heard about a big-city cop. These are the facts, ma'am. The skipper there is barely beyond thirty years old. Median age for the whole group could not be much more than twenty-seven or twenty-eight—which put Tom Postum squarely on the median.

Trim, athletic, *rugged*—these were combat troops, not cops. No beer bellies, here—no cigar-chomping, aspirin-gulping, whiskey-guzzling fatcats continually on the make for freebies and feelies—these guys, dammit, were *impressive*!

And this was what the big-city problems had built, in a single generation—from the cop on the beat, with a nightstick and a revolver which was rarely if ever used, to combat troops: grim, hard-eyed young men with tense jawlines and hardrock bellies, Buck Rogers weapons, and every conceivable technological advantage this modern age could offer a threatened society. And still it was not enough.

Something was "going down" out on those streets at this very moment, something really big, and all they could do about it was sit there and stare holes into one another until somebody actually fired a weapon or created a disturbance.

Postum left his stool and went to the window. The skipper watched him for a moment, then said, "Tom ... great work."

"Thanks," Postum replied with a feeble smile. "Not great enough, though, is it?"

A unit head said, "What do you want, Postum? Instant control?"

"Yes. That's what I want," Postum said.

The Skipper told him, "They'll make their move—the wrong move. Then we'll make ours. Action, reaction. Name of the game. Right? Instant control, you've got it."

The intelligence chief turned back to the group at the table. "What bothers me ..."

"Let's hear it," the skipper said, sighing.

"There's a guy running around out there with some sort of exotic equipment. *He* knows what they're doing. *He* knows where they started and where they're headed. *He* knows who they are and where they are."

"So?"

"So why the hell don't *we* know? What makes a guy like Bolan so ... so ..."

"*Omniscient* is your word," the skipper said heavily. "But he's not that. And he's not really the present

60

problem. Part of it, sure, but we had the problem, remember, before we had Bolan. He's just brought things to a head. And I can't really say I mind that."

"What are you going to do about him?" Postum asked quietly.

"Bolan? What else? We're going to shoot him down, just like the order says."

"On sight."

"You've got it."

The intelligence chief's gaze wavered and fell. Bitter words welled into his throat but he was saved from the embarrassment of those by the flash that boomed in on the hotline.

"Explosions and gunfire in Sector Four. Citizen's report. Patrol units responding. We have a pinpoint."

The room was already emptying.

Postum remained behind to assist the skipper with zone assignments.

"There you go, gangbuster," he muttered to the wall. "It's a matter of action and reaction. There's *no* difference between a cop and a soldier."

The wooden signboard marking the narrow road which angled off toward the river had once said something about "auto salvage" but the lettering was weathered and barely discernible now. A decaying wooden fence bounded the property, shielding the metal graveyard within from public view. Small-arms fire was volleying around in there when Bolan hit the scene. The warwagon was parked atop a small mound of earth a few hundred feet on along the main road, opposite the back corner of the fenced enclosure. He pulled the junker alongside and quickly went in for an eyeball conference.

Schwarz was manning the base and advised him, "The police tactical channels are buzzing. Sounds like they're scrambling some heavy stuff—I'd say SWAT teams—probably headed this way if I read their signals correctly."

"They're tracking my hit on the sandwich," Bolan suggested. "I was expecting it. They'll be ranging this way quick enough, though. Where's Pol?"

"He suited up and went in. Maybe a minute ago."

"Is he wired?"

"Yeah."

Bolan punched a digital timer on the console. "There's your mark. Give me two minutes precisely, then drop that fence, over there, right at the corner. Tell Pol. It's all the time we're going to get. Tell him to give me room—I'm punching in. Soon as you drop the fence, roll it and pick us up on your down pass."

He was out the door and running before Schwarz could acknowledge the instructions, delaying at the junker long enough only to hurriedly drape a satchel charge from the hood ornament. Then he was powering into a screaming circle-back and careening into the turn-off to the junk yard.

The gates stood wide open, one lone guy with a shotgun the only thing presuming to bar entry.

The sentry's attention had been going to the developments inside those gates. It was too late for him when he saw that charging vehicle bearing down on him. He was trying to scramble clear and get a charge off at the same time, and he succeeded in neither.

A front fender caught the guy in mid-pirouette with a grazing blow that sent him spinning crazily into the cemetery of dead cars, the shotgun blasting ineffectually into the ground.

The continuing charge sent Bolan's vehicle whining along a circular path between heaps of skeletonized vehicles, and it was not until the final wild curve that he was aware of the ultimate destination of that charge: a dilapidated office-warehouse of wood and stone set into a sea of waste. The three big limousines were pulled up there in a crescent arrangement about fifty feet from the building, and guys were running around behind them waving hardware and making a lot of noise while another group at the end of the building was systematically spreading gasoline and firing the old structure. Already flames were licking high over there—and considering the shape that building was in—the whole thing would be an inferno in a matter of seconds.

All this Bolan assimilated in a flashing microsecond of awareness as that squealing, motorized bomb completed the turn and plunged on toward the congregation of crew wagons. He jammed the gears into neutral and sent the junker into free roll as he bailed out and rolled to cover, with less than a hundred feet of separation between himself and the impact zone.

There was an immediate reaction down there, with guys whirling and yelling and firing reflexively at the driverless car, but it was a classic exercise in futility.

The junker rolled on home to slam broadside into the center crew wagon. The impact charge shook the area and blew a rolling cloud of flame puffing out to engulf vehicles and men and all within a fifty-foot radius, reaching back even to uncomfortably heat the ground-hugging cause of it all.

Guys were screaming and writhing around down there even before the munitions stored in the junker's trunk began unloading in secondary explosions.

Bolan stayed where he lay, pressed to the ground as blast upon blast flailed the atmospheres and welded those four groaning vehicles into a solid ball of fire. Then the gas tanks started, with turreting streamers of liquid fire arcing high in brilliant patterns and raining blazing droplets of rain from hell throughout that tortured zone.

When it was all spent, Bolan hoisted himself upright and made a wary approach, AutoMag at the ready. A figure on the roof of the burning building rose into smoky silhouette and began spraying the fire zone with an automatic weapon. Even at this range and situation, Bolan instantly recognized the stolidly familiar figure of Pol Blancanales—and it was a welcome sight, indeed.

Another blast jarred the area slightly, a relatively distant blast, and The Executioner knew that Gadgets Schwarz also was at work. He gave a high-sign to his compadre on the roof and received a returning signal of recognition.

Men were staggering from the inferno with hands held high—stupefied men with no resistance left in them—choking, coughing, gasping for the breath of life.

Bolan called up, "Pol! Backboard me!"

An "aye aye" floated down from the back side of the roof.

Bolan grabbed a wheezing fat man of about fifty, shook him viciously, and demanded, "Where's Jules?"

The guy's eyes were dazed, uncomprehending. Bolan let him go and turned to another. At that moment, old Jules himself reeled through the smoking doorway and collapsed at Bolan's feet.

There were perhaps a dozen survivors out here, all of them obviously from Pattriccia's force. A younger guy was on one knee, too close to the blazing building, fighting for mere air and giving Bolan a curious gaze.

Bolan grabbed the guy and pulled him clear. "Is this all?" he asked the guy.

The hurting man nodded and wheezed his reply. "Thanks to you, there's this many. I'm Tony Dalton. I owe you, Mister."

Bolan growled, "You owe me nothing, guy. Get these people out of here."

"Did Artie send you?"

"No time for jawing," Bolan growled. "Cops are screaming here from every direction. I'm taking Jules

64

with me. The word is, the rest of you get lost. Go south, and don't hurry back."

"I get you. Thanks."

"Moving out, Pol!" Bolan yelled. He hoisted the old man to his shoulder and headed for the breached fence with all possible haste.

Tony Dalton froze him several paces out with a single, bawling word: *"Bolan!"*

He whirled to that sound with the AutoMag extended.

The guy was just standing there. "You *are* Bolan!"

"I am."

"I don't get it."

"Don't spend the rest of your life worrying about it. Just go!"

"Don't hurt the old man, eh. He's dying anyway."

Bolan spun away from that human moment and went on. Hurting old men was not the name of his Saint Louie game.

He'd come here to slay an idea.

And these old men were going to help him do just that. If, that is, he could make it past these damn St. Louis cops.

Mack Bolan, at that moment, was not at all certain of success in that.

9: ACTION, REACTION

"Tac 1 from Tac 2. Can you *hear* that?"

"Hear it, hell, I can *see* it!"

"Tac 1 from Control. What've you got there?"

"We're at Four Boston Seven, Control. What we have here is a bombed vehicle and seven victims, all DOA. What we have a couple miles up the road is anybody's guess. Can you hear that through my carrier?"

"Affirmative, Tac 1. Sounds like Normandy Beach on D-Day. Can you pinpoint?"

"Negative. Source appears to be in the general vicinity of the old barge works. Column of smoke is now several hundred feet elevation, and explosions are still occurring. We are now rolling to investigate with Tac 2 in company."

"All units, this is Sector Control. Converge on Boston Three, repeating, Boston Three. Exert due caution, this is a possible Maximum Contact. Do not acknowledge, do not acknowledge. Tac 1, you are cleared for Extreme Reaction. Tac 2, you are cleared for Maximum Support. All other units, Sector Four, you are cleared for Maximum Containment and Standby Support. Tac 1 and 2 acknowledge."

"Tac 1 aye."

"Tac 2 aye."

The Sector Leader swiveled away from the console and squeezed the back of his neck as he shot an oblique gaze at the skipper. "Fits Postum's briefing like a picture in a frame," he observed. "The 'bandit' was a tailing vehicle. The guy dropped back and I believe the expression was 'cleared the backtrack.' Now they're having the slug-out up near the old barge docks. I can't fit that into 'wine vat,' though. Can you?"

The skipper shook his head. "Tom?"

Postum said, "I fed winevat to the computer and it spit it back. I guess—"

"Control, this is Tac 1. We're running into dense smoke. Does not appear to be same source as those explosions."

The controller swung back to the console for the response. "Clarify, Tac 1."

"We're into a—a *smoke screen,* I believe. Visibility is near zero."

The skipper cussed. Tom Postum pulled up a chair and straddled it.

"What is your situation, Tac 1?"

"Proceeding at maximum allowable speed. That's about, uh, five miles per hour—and it's getting worse."

"Tac 4, Tac 4, this is Control!"

"Tac 4 aye."

"Report!"

"Tac 4 is now approaching Alpha Three."

"This is Control, Tac 4 is cleared for Extreme Reaction. Tac 5 is cleared for Maximum Support. Both acknowledge."

"Tac 4 aye."

"Tac 5 aye."

The Sector Leader turned to the skipper with a scowl. "Smart bastards," he growled.

"Well if *our* people can't see, neither can *they*," the skipper philosophized.

"Maybe," Postum softly commented.

"What do you mean, *maybe*?"

"I simply mean—"

"Control, Tac 4—we're in it now, too. Visibility about ten feet maximum."

The controller swore, "Goddamnit!" then viciously kicked his talk bar. "Tac 3, report!"

"Tac 3 aye, converging along coordinate three, midway between Alpha and Boston. Control, I am also socked in."

"Well kiss my ass!" the sector leader yelled.

"Seal it off!" the skipper snarled. "I'll bring you help from the other sectors."

"This is Sector Four Control! All units are cleared for Extreme Reaction. This is a Maximum Contact, repeating, this is a—"

Postum had leapt from his chair to interrupt the broadcast. "You're not getting out, Larry!"

"What?"

"Look at your modulators, dammit!"

The controller stared stupidly at his transmission monitor then released the console foot bar, thus freeing the squelch control. A cacophony of squeals and squawks, rapidly alternating across the entire audio spectrum, instantly swirled in through the speakers.

"What the *hell* is *that*?" the controller yelled.

"You're being jammed!"

"I'm being *what*?"

"Someone is operating a jamming device on this channel!"

The skipper called over from another sector: "We're getting it here, too!"

Postum called out, "Switch to your secondaries!"

"No good," Sector Four reported miserably. "How can they do this? How do they jam all frequencies at once?"

"With great difficulty," Postum marveled.

The skipper yelled, "What the hell kind of gear do those bastards *have* out there!"

The intelligence chief was suddenly grinning like an idiot. "I really couldn't say," he told his skipper. "I really haven't the faintest fucking idea."

And he did not particularly give a damn, either.

The warwagon was navigating through her own smoke via a system of "Laser-augmented infrared" optics, and it was a mind-boggler for Pol Blancanales. He occupied the copilot position to Bolan's right, staring with awe into the small viewscreen of the command console.

Schwarz was manning the Electronic Counter Measures gear in the waist, although Bolan himself could just as easily have handled that chore from the command deck.

Blancanales said, "This is giving me vertigo. It's like one of those trick driving machines in the penny arcades, the road just rolling up in front of you in that little box. How fast we going?"

"Twenty," Bolan grunted.

"Damn!"

"The trick is to keep your crosshairs centered and your brakes ready. We'll be breaking clear soon."

"This is the damnedest smoke. What'd you call it?"

"Heavy gas," Bolan replied absently, concentrating on his navigation. "Has a dispersal ratio of roughly a million to one. Reaches that level very quickly then goes inert and heavy, just lays there. In heavy winds, of course, it's not so effective."

"Impressive, very impressive," his companion said.

"How's Jules?"

"Sucking oxygen and cussing. So far he's hung Ciglia on a meat hook, drawn and quartered him, baked him, and served him to the *commissione* for appetizers. When I came forward, he was working on Augie Marinello for the main course."

Bolan chuckled. "Seventy-five years old," was his comment.

"Yeah, well, personally I—huh *ho*! Is that clear air I see swirling out there?"

Bolan replied, "It is. Get set for the worse. Smoke's all gone. We're on our own, now."

"Uhhh . . . yeah, yeah! There's the Interstate! What is that—I-70?"

"It'd better be," Bolan replied grimly. He was accelerating rapidly, now, moving toward an access road which paralleled the interstate route. He called back to the waist: "Gadgets! Situation!"

"Looks clear to me, Sarge."

"Okay, we're home free," Bolan announced. He swung the big rig through an underpass and around a cloverleaf to the southbound side of the freeway and onto the ramp. "Secure ECM," he called to Schwarz.

Blancanales lit cigarettes and handed one to Bolan. The weary blitzer accepted it with a grin and admitted, "That was too close."

"Looked mighty sweet to me," Schwarz said, coming forward. "Where the hell did you get this gear? I never saw such—you've got a tandem-driven saturation-pulse FM mixer pushing a broad-band demodulating scanner back there. Did you know that?"

Bolan grinned at Blancanales and said, "Is that what it is?"

"Best I can figure, it is," Schwarz solemnly replied. "I'd have to really go into it to really—of course, it could be—well, let's see. You're whipping those driven scanners across all the—you see, it's a spectrum tuner,

71

double-ganged to the—what're you grinning about, Pol?"

"Just trying to relate it to something I understand," Blancanales replied, winking at Bolan. "I guess it's like making love, eh?"

"I don't see how," Schwarz replied soberly.

"Well sure. Double-ganged impulse-actuated mutual orgasm, Gadgets—detumescing down to a single-pole push-pull disconnect. Universal joint, see."

"That sounds like double-talk," Schwarz said, hung between a smile and a frown. "You see, in frequency-modulated jamming concepts, what you're doing is setting up a—"

"Get outta here!" Blancanales growled.

"You've got no sense of harmony, Pol," Gadgets said soberly.

"A robot! A damned computer! With frizzy control circuits and kinky transistors! And weak tubes! I never saw such a solid-state freak in all my life! You and your damned *contacts*!"

Schwarz was grinning amiably. "See, this stuff is all interrelated. There's a harmony, a unity in nature, and I understand that. You don't, Pol, and you don't even want to, and that's your problem. You're afraid of nature."

"What's this have to do with making love?" Blancanales snarled.

"It's got nothing to do with it. That's what I—"

"Well thank Jesus! He finally admitted it!"

"Admitted what? I'm talking about the . . ."

Bolan was grinning hugely, savoring these relaxed few moments with the closest thing he'd known to "family" through many a long campaign. But that relaxation was to be short-lived.

He cruised past the huge Gateway Arch at the foot of town and was angling into the interchange to I-44, on a deadline course for "Stonehenge," when the beeper began signaling an incoming call on the mobile telephone.

"What's that?" Blancanales asked, abruptly dropping the tension-relieving banter.

"Telephone," Bolan said.

"Who the hell would be calling?"

"I'd really rather not find out," Bolan told him, with a sober smile.

But the thing kept beeping.

"Maybe it's Toni," Blancanales said, worrying about that. "Does she know—"

Bolan sighed. "Yeah, she knows. Better get it. Do it cool, though."

Blancanales picked up the instrument and identified the mobile number, then frowned and said, "Just a minute." He showed Bolan an apologetic grimace as he reported, "Long distance. Guy wants to talk to La Mancha."

Bolan made the exchange onto I-44 then reached for the instrument. "La Mancha here," he said, using his street voice.

The troubled tones of Leo Turrin, another member of this "family," told him, "I really did not want to make this call, Sarge."

"So why did you?"

"Because there's a guy named Bolan standing here with a gun at my head."

"Say again?"

"You heard me right," said the best friend Mack Bolan had ever known. "His name is Bolan, and he wants you in the very worst way."

And that's the way it was, sometimes, in Mack Bolan's world.

10:   STANDING ROOM

"It's the kid brother," Turrin explained with an unhappy sigh. "I think he's flipped out. He's got this shiny new Colt .45 which he assures me is loaded and ready—and frankly, Sarge, I think it must run in the family, he's giving me the shivers. I figured, uh, I'd better just make the call."

Bolan said, "Sorry, Leo. Put him on."

"No, he won't accept that. Guess he's afraid he'll get talked out of it."

"Out of what?"

"He wants an eyeball meet. Yesterday, if not sooner."

"Leo, I can't—I'm in the middle of a thing here."

"Sure. Johnny and the whole world knows it. He still wants that meet. And I, uh, I think we better try to work it out."

Bolan gave a despairing sigh. "Doesn't sound like Johnny, Leo. He must have a tough one."

"Well, to tell the truth, there have been some, uh, surprising developments on the local scene. He says he'll blow my damn head off if I whisper a word to you about it. Wants to do that, himself, eyeball to eyeball."

Bolan's heart leapt. "Something happened to Val?"

"Uh, naw, no—not like that. Look, I can get a plane in about an hour. Let me bring him out. Forget the gun and take my word for it. He needs. We can handle it, can't we?"

Bolan's decision was typically immediate. "Okay. Double cover your tracks. Put some dark glasses on him and keep them there. Johnny knows the game and how to play it but you'd better give him a quick refresher. There's a motel at the airport. Check in there under your own name. Go straight to the room and stay there until I make contact. What time do you expect to arrive?"

"Let's say mid-afternoon."

"Right. I'll get there at the earliest possible. Tell Johnny I say right now, he's to give you the hardware."

"Yeah, uh . . . okay. I have it. He says to tell you he has *not* flipped out. And uh, shit, this is a BB pistol, Sarge. Sure looked like the real article to me."

Bolan grinned. "Tell him to hang in there. I trust him, and I understand. I'll see you both as soon as I can carve a trail. And Leo . . . thanks."

"Knock it off. Just say goodbye."

"Goodbye, Leo."

Bolan handed the phone to Blancanales and told him, "Personal problem. I'm going to have to work it in, somehow."

"Brother John."

"Yeah."

Schwarz was seated on the floor between the two, his back against the command console. "He wrote me once, in 'Nam. Cindy, too. I'm sorry, I never got

76

around to answering. I'm not much on that. What's he now—about sixteen?"

"Try sixty," Bolan said quietly.

"Raw deal," Blancanales said, commenting on the Bolan family tragedy.

"I didn't do much to lighten it," Bolan said, scowling. "I was all he had left. Then I took even that away from him."

"The kid understands," Blancanales said, trying for reassurance.

"Understanding is one thing—living with it, something else," Bolan said softly. "John and I talked about it. Before I declared war. Sure, he's a gutsy kid. He understood what would happen, and he cheered me on. Still does. But . . . hell, it must be a grim life for a kid like that."

Schwarz said, "My folks died while I was in 'Nam. They were pretty old. But I still ache, sometimes."

Blancanales gave his partner a searching gaze. "I didn't know that, Gadgets."

The electronics genius shrugged. "I was a change-of-life baby. Their one and only. My dad proudly gave me his name, the whole thing—and Mama gave me her life, what there was left of it. Then Uncle Sam stepped in and took it all. I was a draftee. Did you know that? Mama wanted me to go to Canada. I almost did. But my dad would have had a heart attack for sure. He was a patriot, a double-deuce vet, American Legion and all that. So, hell, I went to 'Nam. And I re-upped over there. Didn't even get home for their funeral. Didn't even get the word until two weeks after." He grinned solemnly and went on in that matter-of-fact tone. "I was shagging the black gang along the Ho Chi Minh Trail."

"They died together?" Bolan asked, perhaps relating the experience to his own.

"Day apart. Mama first. She died in the bed they'd shared for forty-two years. Died in her sleep. Guess my dad just couldn't get over the shock. Had a bad heart. They had a thing, those two. Dad always said he'd never live to see them put her in the ground. And he didn't."

Blancanales sighed. "Of all the crazy things we've talked about . . . and you're just now getting this in. I didn't know you had aches, Gadgets."

"Cycle of life," Schwarz said, grinning suddenly. "It all ties in somewhere, back at some power source. We're just so many carrier modulations, see, running along a PC board and—"

"Don't do that," Blancanales said, soberly interrupting. "It's good to let it hang out, sometimes. Don't keep it stuffed into those spaghetti circuits all the time."

Schwarz gave his old friend an embarrassed smile and went aft.

"There's a deep one," the Pol said quietly.

"Yeah," Bolan agreed.

The sober moments had apparently produced an unsettling effect. Blancanales chewed the back of his hand for a moment, then blurted, "I'm worried as hell about Toni, Sarge."

Bolan sighed.

"I shouldn't have allowed her into this company. God, she's young, too. And what kind of life is this for a woman?"

Bolan said, "She told me the story, in New Orleans. I think she knows what she's doing. Women need fulfillment, too, Pol. Some of them can't find it with a ring and a promise. You may as well face it—I believe Toni is our kind. Val, now . . ."

"I heard you mention her name on the phone. I didn't want to pry, but—what's happening?"

Bolan shook his head. "I'll know when Johnny gets

here. I was assured otherwise but somehow I can't shake the feeling that this crisis or whatever involves Val. She and Johnny have been like brother and sister ever since—well, I don't know. I've never liked the idea of tying those two together. Johnny's neck is in my noose—and there's no way out of that, now. Val's wouldn't have to be there. I've tried many times to release her and she just won't release. But Val is not the kind to—Val needs a ring and a promise, Pol. I could never give her that. The only ring she'll ever wear on my behalf will be a mourning band. And the only promise will be carved on a headstone."

The Politician sighed. "I think Gadgets has the right idea. Keep it buried. Guys like us have no right to ... You're right too, you know. If you stand, you stand alone. Otherwise it just gets too damned confused. But I'd still like to check on Toni."

Bolan's gaze flicked to the mobile phone. "Give her a call. Let it ring twice only, then disconnect. Call again immediately and repeat the routine. She'll pick up on the third call."

Blancanales smiled apologetically and instituted the routine.

Bolan concentrated on the route and began watching for exit directions, visions of Johnny and Val playing lightly just beneath the surface of his mind.

Del Annunzio's hardsite in Webster Groves was now only minutes away. Annunzio himself had been leading the charge on Jules Pattriccia. But the hardsite was still there. The battle plan called for a quick haymaker to that vital organ before there could be any concerted recovery from the disaster at Winevat. Everything else would have to stand aside until that important objective had been achieved. The numbers simply would allow no deviation.

But the depths of Mack Bolan were churning with the

unhappy and potentially disastrous developments *vis à vis* Johnny Bolan's insistence upon an audience with the warrior in the midst of battle.

Both Johnny and Val had been kept in low-profile protective concealment since the moment Bolan had put Pittsfield behind him. Their lives were in great danger. The mob would whack them just for simple retaliatory pleasure—or there could be a duplication of the Boston nightmare, when the two had been snatched in an effort to force Bolan into the open.

Leo Turrin had proven to be the greatest friend those two could ever hope for—and virtually their guardian angel. As the underboss of the Pittsfield arm, he had instant and direct access to whatever may be going down in the area. As an undercover federal cop, he had the official clout to keep the pair under the most stringent security precautions.

Bolan had decided long ago that the very best thing that he personally could do for them was to get out of their lives and stay out. Of course, that could sometimes prove difficult.

Johnny should not have slapped leather on faithful Leo—not even toy leather. That was an immense breach of ethics—and Johnny certainly realized that truth as strongly as did Bolan himself.

So, sure, something was terribly out of focus in Pittsfield. And, moments later, Pol Blancanales added nothing whatever to the peace of Bolan's subsurface worries.

"It's no good," he reported fretfully. "I worked the combination exactly and now the damn thing is ringing off the wall. She's not answering, Sarge."

And *that* was not like *Toni*!

A muscle worked in Bolan's jaw as he softly replied, "She's standing, Pol."

"What?"

"While we take Stonehenge, Toni is standing. She's

one of us. We'll check her out as soon as we can. Until then . . ."

"Yeah," Blancanales growled. "She stands alone."

There was, unhappily, no other way to stand.

11:   CALLING IT

"Stonehenge" was situated on the eastern edge of a suburban community, a semi-rural estate which had once been the heart of a productive and prosperous farm—most of whose acreage had long ago been sub-divided and developed for "country executive" living—presumably for those who found the confinement of city life unpleasant and who had the means to escape it.

Stonehenge was a code name, of course, assigned by Gadgets Schwarz to the stone-walled, fortress-like cluster of ancient buildings which remained as the only link to an agricultural past. The house itself was huge and impressive, obviously put there by someone with strong cultural ties to European traditions and possessing a fondness for baronial estates. Structured from native stone and whole logs, it rose to three full stories and a mansard roof complete with "widow's walk" in an open cupola.

Various incidental outbuildings were clustered to the

rear, all of those also of stone except for a relatively new wooden horse barn and corral. The surrounding terrain inside the walls was more or less flat with here and there a gentle knoll to break the monotony, a stand of oak or willow—ten acres of "country executive" living at its best.

The subdivision lay off to the west and south, the boundaries well marked by a dense stand of trees which followed the entire line and provided a second, outer "fence" for the walled estate.

Title to the property had recently been transferred to an outfit calling itself "Mid-Missouri Mortgage Holding Company"—a subsidiary of "Midwest Mortgage Bankers Group, Inc."—itself a corporate structure within "American Associates Holding Corporation" whose primary cash assets reposed in Swiss banks and were manipulated solely by the circle of iron old men in New York known to law enforcement officials everywhere as *La Commissione*.

Stonehenge was a hardsite, pure and simple.

It was, evidently, destined to become the official capitol of the new midwestern empire now being so carefully staked out on the Missouri plain by those ruthless old men whose domain already extended from sea to shining sea across this land which had long ago forsaken baronial ideas and feudal dreams.

Mack Bolan was *damned* if they were going to get away with it.

The often romantically touted Mafia idea was, in fact, nothing but a diehard echo from the jungles of survival which most enlightened peoples had abandoned generations ago.

Stonehenge was a standing symbol of that echo.

The Mafia motif was, in effect, a feudal system based upon the supposition that the strongest and meanest man around deserved to be the "chief"—the head man—the *king*—and that all others should accept his beneficence as and when he wished to dispense it.

To the worthy would be deeded fiefs of their own, and these in turn would sublet small plots of turf (or "territories") for lesser lieges.

Of course, the larger benefits accruing in such a pyramidal system typically went to the man at the top of the pyramid—and the maintenance of that pyramid required the constant use of force, fear, intimidation, terror.

It was not a very democratic idea.

But it was a very ancient one.

The chief difference between a genuine feudal system and the Mafia version lay in the angle of approach.

In a nation politically constituted under such a system, the man at the top was indeed a king or emperor, a sheik or a czar, a *fuehrer* or a *duce*. The raping of a nation and a people went on in the full glare of daylight and under the laws of the land.

In a land where the laws frowned on such behavior, the pyramid could operate only in an inverted fashion, the apex buried deeply underground beneath layer upon layer of "support" gradually building to the surface for a "base" that oozed into every nook and crevice in the upper world that would admit it and allow it to flourish. It was an upside-down pyramid.

Hence, the term "underworld."

The old-world Mafia had once been a sort of poorman's aristocracy, the result of a slave revolt by desperate men who replaced official tyranny with a homespun version of their own. It was perhaps not too reprehensible an idea for a time and place where a systemized looting and raping of the powerless was an official way of life.

This "aristocracy," however, represented the degeneration of a purer idea.

The earlier "Society of Matthew" (from the Latin,

Matthew: brave, bold) was based on a sort of Robin Hood idea. Early *mafiosi* stole back from the rich that which had been legally extracted from the poor, spread terror, and exacted tribute throughout the landed and monied gentry—and began to restore some measure of justice to the common folk of the time.

It is probably true, however, that power corrupts—and that absolute power corrupts absolutely. With the growing success of the Mafia brigands, the reins of terror and oppression were merely transferred from the official fiefs to the underground ones—or shared mutually. The common citizen often found himself squeezed between two masters—one exploiting him from the top, the other from the bottom.

The two-headed pyramid of power was thus complete—one the mirror image of the other, each side sharing a common base—upon the backs of the people—an apex in both the upper and under worlds. The one systematically aided and abetted the other, each protected the other, and the peasants found their burdens doubled rather than diluted.

Bolan was well aware of Mafia history.

And he was thoroughly repelled by the disgusting philosophy that embraced social cannibalism as a "smart" way of life while sneering at every decent and uplifting movement of mankind.

In his war journal, he had once written:

"These guys do not build anything. They just destroy. Sometimes they destroy for the sheer joy of it, but usually it is due to common greed linked with a total lack of reverence for anything noble or constructive. They're like greedy dead-end kids turned loose to shift for themselves at a birthday feast of cake and ice cream: they'll smash the cake and splatter the banquet room with ice cream, rip down the decorations, and turn the whole party sour—then walk away with a smirk and a strut because they got more than the "dopes." And if they do build anything at all, it is only toward another smirk and strut."

Yes, Mack Bolan understood his enemy.

They were "stone-agers"—primitives who would keep the world a jungle for as long as decent men turned the other cheek or tried to contain them by civilized methods.

There was but one way to deal with a primitive.

You met him at his own terms, on his own ground, with his own methods—the only kind he would ever truly understand and respect. Then you simply eliminated him from the civilized world and returned him to the age where he belonged.

You killed the bastard.

Bolan knew that game, knew it well, and the moment had arrived for Stonehenge.

Gadgets Schwarz had been designated "base support"—a role for which he was now receiving a final briefing as the other two suited up.

"Soon as you drop us, get it up to the high ground and institute optic and radio surveillance. Pol and I are wired, but let's have radio silence except for absolute urgencies. If you get a sniff of blues, sound the alert and stand by for evasive disengage. If something else shows, send the word then lay low and quiet it. Leave it to Pol and me to play the reaction."

Schwarz nodded in understanding. "Okay. What about the fire assignment?"

"If we need fire support, we'll call it in by the grid. Looking straight at the main building from your position, dead center will be 'Fire One.' Every click left of center will be a progressive even number—Fire Two, Fire Four, and so on. Right of center gets a progressive odd number."

"Okay."

"For elevations, count odd for each click above center, even for below."

"Got it. Like, if I'm sending two clicks left and two down, you'll call it Fire Four Four."

"Right. You also have the option for free fire, Gadgets, and I leave that to your own head. Just be damn sure you know what you're firing on. Also, they're big rockets and there's only four to the pod, so don't spend them cheaply."

"Yeah, I read that. Hey—you guys don't do anything wild."

Blancanales rolled his eyes at that.

Bolan grinned sourly and said, "Let's go see what they have."

12:   THE FOLLOWER

The skipper had grabbed a tactical scout 'copter to rush
to the scene of disaster, and he'd invited the intelligence
boss to accompany him—but Tom Postum demurred,
preferring to follow more sedately, and perhaps more
thoughtfully, in his lumbering electronic reconnaissance
van.

The "smoke screen" had cleared out and the scene
was straight out of the tactical training manual when he
arrived. Grim-faced and heavily armed young SWAT
cops in flak jackets were deployed in hard containment
teams wherever the practiced eye could see along the
approaches to the combat zone. A mobile base unit
with direction-finder antenna patiently rotating was
pulled onto the relatively high ground across the road
from the old salvage yard. Small scout teams were
moving vigorously in both directions along the fence,

and everywhere lay the heavy atmosphere of grim purpose and official determination.

But Tom Postum knew that it was already too late for any of that. He pulled in beside a Quick Reaction Vehicle and caught the eye of the unit leader who was standing disconsolately alongside. He recognized the cop as "Four Unit One."

"What went?" Postum asked him.

The young sergeant shook his head and made a wry face. "Some damned fancy footwork," he replied. "Skipper's inside, Lieutenant. Don't get too close to him, though. His vibes are approaching critical mass."

Postum winked solemnly and eased his van past another couple of QRVs which were parked along the access road. As he swung through the gate, a familiar white sheet marking a somber lump caught his eye off to the right.

"There's *one*," he muttered.

He never got to *two* and *three*—reaching, instead, infinity just around the bend.

"Oh God!" he groaned, upon confronting that sea of DOA markers.

He halted the van and just sat there for a long moment, his mind struggling with the enormity of the thing—the carnage, shattered vehicles, the gutted and charred ruins of a once-sizeable building—and cops, cops everywhere, poking into the post mortem of an Executioner blitz, lab men strolling around, coroner's people running about with wraps and baggies.

A QRV driver came over to stand beside his open window.

"Ever see anything like this, Lieutenant?" the youth asked solemnly.

"Not since a place called My Lai," the intelligence chief replied quietly.

"Oh. You were there?"

"Like now," Postum growled. "After the fact.'"

"Look at those vehicles," the young cop said. "It took a lot of hell to leave them in that shape. Worse junk in the yard, now. I heard the skipper say one of them had been a self-propelled bomb. How could he get that from a mess like *that*?"

"Ask him," Postum replied absently.

"Not me," the kid said, and walked away.

A paramedic team was scrambling around down there in the ruins, hot on the scent of something. Apparently someone had found a live one.

Postum did not wish to see what they would drag from that wreckage. He backed his vehicle around and went out of there. He turned right onto the main road and slowly followed the fence line to the gaping hole at the northwest corner, then stopped again and got out for a closer look.

It was obviously a fresh break—and, just as obviously, a small explosive charge had done the work.

A SWAT cop standing there apologetically told him, "Sorry, sir, this area is sealed for the lab team."

Postum nodded his head, accepting that without comment, and walked slowly across the road to a slightly elevated knoll immediately opposite. He found some interesting tire impressions in the soft dirt there, grunted, then straightened up with hands on hips to meticulously survey the hit zone from this point of view.

The intelligence man grunted again then, and returned to his vehicle. He went into the van and ran a plotline to the point of last-known radio contact, then bracketed the "smoke zone" and ran a few more plotlines.

Sourpuss Postum was not grinning now. He may never, in fact, do so again.

He went forward and sent the vehicle into motion again, U-turning along the backhaul and rolling slowly, seeking an inconspicuous and probably little-used trail cross-country.

He found it, less than a quarter-mile along—a backcountry dirt road bearing away from the delta lowlands and pointing the way westward.

A few minutes later, he found himself staring at an access ramp to Interstate 70. Again he consulted his graph and again he frowned.

He called in to headquarters and told his watch commander: "Willis, this is priority hot. I want you to get me a computer program access into a historical bank—or maybe anthropological. Tell them what we want and let the experts figure it out. Maybe you should query first Washington University. If they can't supply it, they should be able to put us onto someone who can."

"Yes, sir. What's the query?"

"Stonehenge." He spelled it. "That's the site of some ancient Druidic ruins somewhere in England. Here's the cross-check I want. I want something in the St. Louis metro area which could relate, either historically or physically—or both—to Stonehenge."

"Got it. You'll be in the mobile, Lieutenant?"

"I will. I'm on Interstate 70 about three miles north of Jefferson Memorial, rolling south, following my smell. Get me that data with all possible haste."

"Will do."

Postum returned the mike to its clip and activated the scan monitors. He was following more than a smell.

The chief of police intelligence knew that he was following a brilliant military mind—and a highly dangerous one.

That scene back there at the salvage yard had jarred Tom Postum's conscience. This was not some silly damned tactical game of point and counterpoint.

A dangerous military force was conducting an illegal war on this turf—a scorched-earth war, the likes of which had not been seen in this land since the War Between the States.

And, yes, Postum was following more than a smell. He was following a shiver and a certainty.

13:   OLD TIMES

Pol Blancanales walked nonchalantly through the gate at the front of the estate and along the winding drive toward the house.

He was in combat fatigues, with web belts crossing the chest and encircling the waist, a small machine gun dangling from a neck cord, an M-16 rifle slung jauntily from the right shoulder.

About fifty yards in, a distant and disturbed voice faintly called, "Hey! You, guy!"

A skinny man with a wolfish dog dragging him along at the end of a short leash was hurrying across the lawn toward him, from the area of the north wall. The guy was dressed in denim jeans and plaid shirt, hardware visible at the hip in open leather.

In the background of that vision, a figure in black had just slithered over the top of the wall and dropped lightly to the ground inside.

Blancanales smiled and stepped over to a willow

sapling, turned his back on all that, opened his fly, and began casually watering the tree.

The guy and the dog were upon him before that task was completed.

"What the hell is this?" the guy asked angrily while the dog sniffed suspiciously at the fresh moisture on the ground.

"Takin' a leak," the Pol amiably explained.

"I can see that!" The sentry was eyeing those weapons. "What is this? What're you doing in here?"

Blancanales smiled benignly and replied with a question of his own. "Why are you standing here jawing when you got a dead man up there on the gate?"

The guy's face went dumb, scared, and unbelieving all at once. "Ringo? Ringo's *dead*?"

The Blancanales smile was pure "aw shucks" charm. "Yeah. I just now did it to 'im."

A muscle popped in the guy's jaw and his eyes flared noticeably one telegraphic second before he went for his gun.

The Pol's left hand flashed up and across, a mere inch of surgical steel protruding therefrom and slashing the wrist of that impotent gunhand then traveling on up in the cross-slash to open a frothing welt at the throat.

The dog danced away in surprise to clear that gurgling fall, then crouched with fangs bared in attack mode.

A long-bladed hunting knife leapt into the Pol's hand. He waved it menacingly in front of that slavering snout while sternly commanding, "Down! Down, damn you, or I'll spill you!"

It was about a ten-second staredown before the beast tucked its tail and settled uncertainly to the ground, undecided between a snarl and a whimper.

Pol put out a cautious hand to scratch that dangerous head, then he seized the leash and gently urged the animal to his feet.

"Let's go, pooch," he said, setting off again for the house at a leisurely pace, the dog in tow with not so much as a backward glance for his fallen handler.

He was challenged again less than a hundred feet from the house. The challenger was under the cupola on the roof, practically invisible along this line of sight, and he was throwing down over the telescopic sights of a big rifle.

Blancanales dropped to his haunches beside the dog and peered up at the guy, his mind computing sun angles, firing-line obstructions, ground cover. He was in the open, twenty feet from the nearest possible shelter; the sun was no factor; there were no obstructions confronting the guy on the roof, no blind spots at this range. He was a sitting duck, *he* meaning Rosario Blancanales, the Chameleon, the Politician. Obviously he was not a chameleon in this particular situation. He would have to rely on politics—and perhaps trust and faith in his partner.

"I'm getting sick of this shit," he called up there with a disgusted tone of voice. "Doesn't anybody ever get the word around this joint?"

"Who are you, guy?"

"Who *am* I? Where the hell is the breakfast for my boys? It's two hours late."

"What boys? You sure you got the right camp, kid?"

"Aw, come on, dammit! Get that cannon off of me!"

The guy up there was wavering. "Where's Al?"

"Al who?"

"You've got his dog, guy."

"Oh. Him. He went up to the gate to talk to Ringo. You can't see that from up there?"

"I ain't got stereophonic eyes, guy. I don't see it all at once. How come you've got the dog?"

"He's hungry, like me and my boys. Look, I ain't going to stand here and—"

"Stay put!"

Blancanales had begun a cautious move for the portico. He froze and shouted, "Look, dammit, Del promised to send some chow out two hours ago!"

The guy lifted off the scope but the bore of that rifle remained dead center. "I ain't heard nothing about no company of grunts outside the walls."

"You saw me come in, didn't you!"

"Sure."

"Well, dammit, Ringo has the word. Al has the word. I know the housemen have the word 'cause they're supposed to be feeding us. Now dammit . . ."

It had been a long parley. Where the hell was—

The guy up there was saying, "You stay put. I'm calling down to send someone out."

"It's about time!"

"Don't get smart!" It looked as though the guy had a phone to his ear now. "What're you made up for, guy, Hallowe'en or something?"

"There's a war on, dummy, in case you hadn't noticed," Blancanales growled back.

"I never noticed you before, guy."

"Just make the call. Tell 'em it's breakfast for the barf squad and where the hell is it!"

"What squad was that?"

"Barf! Barf! Like a dog makes with a B in front!"

The guy laughed and called back, "Just a min—" but he was overstating his time limitations. That guy did not have a minute left. He had suddenly gone stiff, and Blancanales could see—even at this range—those eyes bulging in a very characteristic manner.

Man and gun disappeared inside the cupola.

A moment later, a familiar figure in black appeared briefly to send down a hand signal.

Man and dog proceeded casually on, arriving at the steps to the big stone porch just as the front door opened.

A big guy stepped outside, pistol in hand, fixing that alien presence out there with a hard stare.

"What's all the yawping about? What the *hell* are you?"

"Look, I'm just not going through that all over again," Blancanales testily replied. He draped the wrist loop of the dog leash over the spire of a low, wrought-iron railing then turned his back on the guy to give the dog a farewell pat.

When he came up and around, the chattergun was in his hands and blazing.

The burst swept the big guy off the porch and head first into a freshly dug flower garden at the edge of the lawn.

Another burst atomized the glass panels framing the door as the warrior took those broad cement stairs in two leaping strides and hit the doorway at full gallop, bursting inside with the auto at full chatter—catching two guys in the entry hall with mouths wide open and hardware barely clear of leather, sweeping them together like so much rubbish into a tumbled welter of arms and legs and depositing them in a corner near the far doorway.

The room just beyond was a huge, ballroom-like affair with vaulted ceilings and a magnificent curving stairway. That particular area was clear of human presence at the moment, but just beyond was another broad hallway with tall sliding doors along either side—and a guy was hurtling out of one of those rooms as the Pol reached the center of the ballroom.

This guy had a chopper and they dueled briefly—very briefly—with a stream of big forty-five-calibre slugs chewing a path past Blancanales' feet before he could hang a wreath of steel jackets around that chest down there.

At that same instant, a heavy weapon which could only be Big Thunder boomed and reverberated along the stairwell to herald the appearance of another body, this one in free fall from somewhere above. Man and weapon crashed to the tiles at Blancanales' feet.

He yelled up, "Watch it, there—you damn near got me."

"You watch it," Bolan's icy tones called down. "There's more of the same up here, between you and me."

The big man in black was obviously on the top floor.

"Secure level one," he instructed the Pol. "I'll take care of this."

A couple of yappy revolvers came alive immediately, up there, as Blancanales skirted around the stairwell and went on through to check out the rest of the main floor.

A thunderous duel was going on above his head as he went through the rooms at ground level, and he was starting down the darkened stairs to the basement when Bolan appeared at the kitchen door.

"How many outsiders, Pol?" the big grim man asked him.

"I took out the gateman and the north sector wall," he replied casually.

"I guess that does it, then. The whole cadre must be out headhunting. These guys were stationkeepers."

"I was just about to check out the basement."

"Lock it and leave it, for now," Bolan said. "I'll get to it. Let's find the family jewels."

Blancanales grinned. "Through the ballroom, down the east hall, first sliding door to your left. I'll show you."

It had probably once been a combination library-study, and very impressively so. Now it was a garishly decorated business office with life-sized *Playboy*-style pinups framed and hanging behind glass from the cherrywood paneling—a massive hardwood desk with a

100

heavy conference table butted against it in a *T* arrangement, overflowing ashtrays everywhere.

It smelled like a bar in there.

Where once had been bookshelves was now a massive wall of unrelieved steel. It was a bank-style vault.

"Paydirt," Bolan murmured and went immediately to the vault.

He had a load of plastics in a heavy ready-bag which hung from a shoulder strap. He placed the bag on the floor and began kneading long strips of the stuff and deftly shaping it into door wedgies.

This operation always gave Blancanales the shivers.

"I'd better keep watch," he suggested, and wandered out to the ballroom.

The skydiver from upstairs was crumpled there at the bottom of the stairwell with dead eyes widely staring, grotesque in his death with limbs poking out at weird angles, a hole the size of a fist behind one ear—a soggy, messy corpse but better company than a bag of goop and that big, grim guy massaging it around that way.

Blancanales trudged around the lower level, peering out windows and whistling softly to himself for several minutes. Then the big guy came out, grinning soberly and fiddling with a small black box he wore on his readybelt.

"Better take cover," Bolan warned. "I want to get it the first try. Might take the whole room with it."

They stood at the back side of the stairwell while Bolan punched the button on the black box to trigger the detonators in the goop—and yeah, it was a pretty good blow, but it did not take the whole room with it.

It did spring the vault door, though—barely—and the goodies inside were well worth the Pol's uneasy stomach.

Bolan was inspecting the blast marks at the heavy

door. "This must be an old one," he marveled. "Not like the usual shoeboxes you find today."

Blancanales grunted with obvious disdain and went directly to the back wall, where an entire shelf was stacked high with bundles of American currency—in twenties, fifties, and hundreds.

He whistled softly. "Well look at that. Must be a couple hundred thousand here."

Bolan glanced at the fortune in American green and said, "Take it. That's gun money. They won't be needing it now."

Blancanales chuckled and snared a leather suitcase from another shelf.

Bolan was conducting a rapid search through stacks of papers, metal boxes, odds and ends of stuff.

The Pol filled the leather bag and tossed it into the room. "See any film?" he asked the big guy.

"Yeah. Some sixteen-millimeter stuff in that metal box by the door. The big one."

Bolan had evidently found his prize. He straightened up with a bundle of bound ledgers in his hands, grinning.

Blancanales was bending over the big metal box. He exclaimed, "Hell! I think this is it! It *is*!"

"Cut a few feet from each reel," Bolan suggested. "It should be enough to satisfy your client. Dump the rest on the floor and we'll torch it."

"Good idea," the Pol agreed, and went to work with his knife. "I'll try to pry a few labels off these cannisters, too."

Moments later they were standing outside the vault with their booty. Bolan passed his old buddy an incendiary and told him, "You took the big risks—you get the honors."

Blancanales grinned, accepted the incendiary, activated it, and tossed it into the vault—then banged the door on the whole dismal business.

"Let's get out of here," he muttered. "This joint is giving me the creeps."

"Wait for me on the porch," Bolan told him, when they reached the ballroom, "I'm going below for a few minutes."

"For what?"

"I brought enough goop to drop this whole place. But I have to find the drop points. Take about five minutes, Pol. Are you game?"

Blancanales studied his watch. "We're out of numbers right now. What the hell—let's drop it. I'll eyeball for you from the porch. Hear gunfire, come running."

Bolan smiled soberly, snared his bag of explosives, and went to the basement.

Blancanales wandered out to the porch and lit a cigarette. The dog moaned at him. He went down and removed the leash then told the beast, "Haul ass, guy."

The dog looked at him uncertainly for a moment, the tail alternately wagging and tucking.

"I said *haul ass*! This place isn't fit for man *or* beast!"

The dog slunk away, disappearing a moment later into the trees at the side. Blancanales watched him out of sight, then returned to the porch.

He had just finished his cigarette when the transistor radio on his belt beeped at him.

"Here it comes," he said, sighing, and lifted the bad news to his head. "Go."

Schwarz reported, "Caravan approaching east. Four bandits. One minute."

"Stand by."

He hurried into the house and to the doorway to the basement stairs. "Sarge! Head parties returning! Gadgets says four units, one minute out!"

Bolan called back, "I need a couple more minutes. I think it's worth it. How about you?"

"I'm game."

103

"Tell Gadgets he's got his fire assignment."

"Okay, but it's still going to be hell. Don't screw around down there simply for perfection's sake."

He went back to the porch and relayed the decision to Schwarz, then fed a fresh clip into his chattergun and went down to the lawn to retrieve the M-16.

"Old times are here again," he said aloud to nobody but himself. Then he grinned sourly and walked into the trees to find the best firing alignment.

Old times, yeah.

He'd hid from these bastards long enough—and he was sick of that crap.

It was good to be alive again.

Even if only for a little while.

14:   UNHINGED

Charlie Alimonte was in a terrible mood.

He'd been out scouring the city for hours, looking for something to whack, and he had not drawn a single drop of blood.

Then there'd been that terrible brawl with hot-ass Jerry Ciglia. That damn guy was pure crazy. Couldn't take reality straight from the horse's mouth.

"I'm telling you," Alimonte had assured his boss, "the whole bunch is so dug in we'll never find them. You gave me the dirty end, Jerry. You give Del the only sure thing we have, and you send me out looking for rabbit holes. Well, dammit, there aren't any rabbit holes. Does that make Del a hero and me a clown?"

"We had them *all* yesterday," Ciglia had screamed at him. *"All of them!"*

"Well that was yesterday and this is today. Mack Bolan wasn't snorting around town yesterday. He is today. And I'm telling you, there's not a hole left in town."

Then the lousy shit had called New York, right in Charlie's presence, and told those old men up there that his own head crews weren't worth a shit—told 'em that, right there with Charlie listening to it—worse than that, with some of *Charlie's boys* listening to it!

You couldn't run a head shop *that* way, dammit!

So now other crews were coming in from all around. From Chicago. From Dallas. From Phoenix. From Denver—of all damn places—how humiliating!—reinforcements from *Denver*! From Cleveland, and Cincy, and . . .

Alimonte gnashed his teeth in the memory of it and groaned audibly. His wheelman, Spencer "Indy" Parelli, flicked him a concerned look and said, "You all right, boss?"

"No I'm not all right," Alimonte groused.

"Thinking about, uh—"

"What else? I'd like to squeeze that guy's nuts together. For about two hours straight."

"Yeah," the wheelman said, commiserating with his boss's humiliation.

They had been running in a standard four-wagon formation—closely spaced with two cars ahead and one behind. The head car was now signaling for the turn through the gate, and the following cars were falling back, letting some slack in. Ordinarily this would be a "quick in" maneuver, designed to get all cars inside as quickly as possible once that point car was out of the lineup. If anyone had a mind to do some whacking, it would be a time like this to tempt them the most—with the forces split, half in and half out of home base.

But that point car up there had come to a complete halt and guys were bailing out of there, one running back toward the other vehicles with one hand raised while the others ran around up there by the gate.

Alimonte growled, "What the hell?"

Parelli had stood the car on its nose and shifted into reverse, a purely mechanical response. "Something's sour," he needlessly commented.

"Jim! Tinker! Go see!"

The back doors sprang open and the two jump-seaters hopped out. The guy from the point car was already there, though, leaning in from the wheel man's side to report, "The gate is standing wide open and nobody's there, boss! Wiggy figured—"

"He figured right!" Alimonte assured the guy. "Check it out!"

"We're doing that."

Someone ran into the middle of the road up there and shouted something.

"What was that?" asked Alimonte, frowning.

"They found Ringo the Kid. With a cut throat."

"Inside!" Alimonte decided immediately. "Let's get it inside!"

The guy from the point car jerked his head in a quick nod and ran back up the line, yelling the instruction as he went.

A moment later, the procession lurched ahead then began moving smoothly as car by car swung through the gate and accelerated up the long drive to the house.

Alimonte's face was white with excitement as his own vehicle cleared the gate and lined into the final dash.

"Bolan," he muttered. "It's got to be that Bolan. But how the hell did he find this place?"

"Think he's still here?" Parelli asked, his voice almost breaking with the excitement of the moment.

It had, after all, been a frustrating and anti-climactic day, to this point—and all these boys needed a lift.

"I hope so," Alimonte declared fervently. "God, I hope so."

And, of course, he was.

"It's going to take awhile, Lieutenant," Willis reported. "There are several banks that could be looked into, but nobody's exactly sure where to find them. The man out at the university has sent in a request to the national date center in Washington and hopes to get an index within the next hour or so. Meanwhile, there's only one possibility—and that's the local historical society. The university ran a scan through their stuff and came up with the old McNamara Farms over near Webster Groves. The original land grand was subdivided about ten years ago but the original farm buildings are still there, along with about ten acres of land. The historical society tried to buy the place a few years ago but something went wrong with the deal. They still have the place on their watch list, though. I don't know exactly what the connection is, but the computer evidently found something there in the data to come up with a possible Stonehenge make. Lieutenant? You still there?"

"I'm here, Willis. Who owns the place now?"

"We're checking it out. I'm sorry, that's all I have for now."

"I'm on Route 100 near Rock Hill," Postum said, sighing. "Give me a fix on that farm."

"Say—you're close. McNamara Farms forms the natural extension north of Grove Country Estates. That should be on your map. It's—"

"I have it. Good work, Willis. I'm rolling south. Keep me advised."

"Will do."

The intelligence chief was beginning to feel like a fool. Out here, running around the countryside, grasping at straws and hoping to sniff a fart in a windstorm.

Rock Hill, indeed.

So much for scents and shivers.

So much, also, for computers. Solid-state brains were

108

not the golden panacea which most people seemed to think they were—present company not excepted, he wryly added to that thought. A computer was no smarter than the man sitting at the program board, no more omniscient than the information contained in its data banks, and certainly no more useful than the availability of those banks.

So, the computer was offering him an old farmhouse. Why? Couldn't you ask a computer *how* it arrived at its decisions? Not, probably, without a program code—then that code would require another, and that one another, and on and on into infinity.

But why McNamara Farms? What could be the correlation between ancient ruins in England and—and *what*?

Well *dammit*!

If the historical society was interested, then that could only mean—an ancient ruin? Well, no—the society did not preserve *ruins*.

So what was Stonehenge?

What did it signify to this present age?

What, dammit, *is* it? Program Query: *"Chief Computer—please, sir, what the hell* is *Stonehenge?"*

And from the intelligence chief's personal computer, the one between his ears, came a tentative answer.

Anachronism?

A thing out of time with its surroundings?

An old farm, maybe, all but swallowed up in the march of progress—in the flow of city dwellers back to the countryside?

Postum was shivering again.

And his shivers beat the scanners by about ten seconds. He had just pulled off the road onto a ridge overlooking by perhaps a hundred feet the gently rolling terrain to south and east when the UHF scanner locked onto a signal from an unlikely frequency and his dash-mounted speaker crackled with a brief—oh, so brief—communiqué of a find lately grown so familiar.

A very weak, *"Go."*

And a responding, stronger, *"Caravan approaching, east. Four bandits. One minute."*

"Stand by."

Not the right voice among the two, no, but definitely the right words!

Postum stabbed his chart with a shaking forefinger and quickly related his own position to the brownish patch representing Grove Country Estates.

Hell!

He should be able to *see* it from here!

He grabbed the binoculars and began a scan, then halted almost immediately and refined the focus. An anachronism, yeah. Rising up from lush green fields and stately lines of trees, barely visible from this angle but definitely out of step with place and time—a strongly anachronistic roof with its widow's walk where a lonely housewife could go up and scan the fields for her man—McNamara's woman, maybe—and sure, that was it, a place out of time—the rock walls, the . . .

He put the truck in gear and rolled along the ridge for another few hundred feet, trying for a better angle and finding it. He could see most of it now, even the road running along the eastern boundary and . . . and, yeah, *four damn black limousines* tooling along down there.

Stonehenge revealed! Decoded, discovered . . .

Postum snared his mike from the dashboard clip and was about to report in when the monitor again crackled with another of those cryptic exchanges.

"We're stoning it. Use your own head but don't send another to center. Keep them distant."

"Right. I have acquisition. I have to go. Remain clear of lower grids."

Acquisition of what? Remain clear of ... ? For some reason which Tom Postum would never quite make himself understand, he returned the mike to its clip and stepped outside with the binoculars, remaining close to the vehicle in the hopes of overhearing more but determined also to get a clear look at whatever was going down out there.

The four vehicles had come to a halt outside the wall, tiny figures scurrying around in the focal field of the glasses—unrecognizable through the limited abilities of the glasses but obviously in a state of agitation.

And, from the monitor inside the truck:

"They're looking."

"They've found your welcome home present."

"They're rolling again. One is through . . . two . . . three . . . all birdies now back in the nest. Stand by. Stand by. One away!"

What happened next literally staggered the cop.

The thing came whizzing into the focal field from somewhere eastward, streaking through the air like a blazing arrow and disappearing behind some trees on the Stonehenge grounds ... then a towering fireball mushrooming high above all else down there.

Anachronistic, no—but, *rockets over Missouri?*

It was several seconds before the sound wave reached his ears, confirming the testimony of the eyes with a thunderous, rolling, report ... and by then another blazing arrow was streaking in, another mushroom of fire lifting over the trees ...

Yeah. A military force was waging a war in Missouri!

Then came the capper.

A thin, powdery cloud rose up to partially obscure that ancient roof down there—and the roof, Mrs. McNamara's walk and all, slipped away and descended within the cloud below the trees.

111

Postum dropped the glasses and scrambled to his vehicle.

Stonehenge was not merely decoded.

Stonehenge was now unhinged.

15: WHEELING IT

Bolan joined Blancanales in the trees out front and re-lieved him of the M-16. They cached their booty from the Stonehenge vault while Blancanales updated him on the outside developments.

"I gave Gadgets firing head," the Pol reported. "He's waiting them into the best target zone. From his angle, that's probably the ninety-degree jog where the drive break's clear of the tree line. That puts them broadside to his firetrack and moving slow along the perpendicular."

Bolan nodded, accepting that. "Complicates our close cover," he commented. "We have to lay high, both of us on the same side. I'll take the point action, you cover the followers. Got some more clips for the '16?"

Blancanales solemnly passed over the backup ammo. "Sarge . . . I'm glad to be back."

"Glad to have you back, Pol."

"Just want you to know. This is, uh . . . it's my own decision to be here. You know?"

Bolan knew. Their gazes locked warmly for a microsecond—and that was all the time there was. The whine of powerful engines in high traction were rapidly approaching—flashes of motion through the trees and reflected sunlight from polished surfaces serving as confirmation of that which was coming at them.

Four cars could mean twenty-five to thirty boys, depending on how well they liked to travel in comfort.

Bolan fingered the black box and hurried off to the point assignment—Blancanales jogging off into the other direction.

He was saving the demolition blast for the best military moment. It would be a ground-shaker, and a further demoralization factor—and there was no doubt in Bolan's mind that he and the Pol were going to need every edge they could manufacture, rockets from on high notwithstanding. Warfare was still primarily a grunt's business and, after all was said and done, it was the eye-to-eye and toe-to-toe that decided most military engagements.

Yeah, Pol. I'm damned glad you're here.

Live large, guy. And, God willing, *live on!*

"Get those windows down!" Alimonte commanded. "Eyes open, and watch your crossfire! Let's don't go shooting each other's ears off. Indy, you stand 'er on the nose at the final tree line! Jim, you and Tinker bail out there and cover the rear. Rest of you boys spring at the parking oval and keep some distance between yourselves! Indy, you stick with the wheels and don't let *no*body come near!"

The wheelman was wondering about the two crews up front. "Yessir. Will Ed and Wiggy—?"

"Standard procedure!" Alimonte snarled. "They'll

cover the sides. Bobby will peel out from the oval and take the rear."

Parelli was lightly tapping his brake pedal now, slowing for the turn onto final approach. He was a true pro, and proud of his status behind the wheel. A good wheelman was worth a dozen guns sometimes. He was critically evaluating the performance of the two in front of him, watching them perform under duress, mentally awarding them both points and brownies depending upon the degree of control and stability exhibited— the way they powered into the turns and recovered into the runs, the smoothness, the . . .

"That's good, good," he muttered.

"What's good?" Alimonte growled, craning his head for a look.

"That turn—did you see that turn? Marty has got—"

"Shut up! Keep your mind!"

Parelli bit his tongue and tapped the brakes again, preparing to seize the moment for a power sweep into that ninety-degree turn left.

He was a trifle upset about Alimonte's sharp words. After all, Parelli was the wheels chief, wasn't he? It was his job to notice such things, to be sure the wheels were always hot and ready to roll, to see that . . .

But then something totally upsetting destroyed his concentration and ruined his timing beyond recovery. Something bright and whizzy came crackling through the air about two car-lengths off to his left, something trailing fire and smoke and moving faster than any competition Parelli had ever been in, something that passed him like he was standing still and whizzed on toward the forward cars which were now running perpendicular to Parelli's course.

Alimonte yelled, *"What the hell?"*

At least, that was what Parelli *thought* the boss yelled. He couldn't be sure—that's how fast that thing was moving. The boss's alarm squeal was eclipsed by the loudest noise ever made on earth, and Wiggy's wheels were completely enveloped in a cloud of fire . . .

And Indy Parelli missed his turn.

It was the crowning humiliation to cap an already humiliating day. The true pro's vehicle was caroming around in the trees. It was all he could do to save the final humiliation—and Indy Parelli did not know nor would he have cared, at that moment, that Ed's wheels had also suddenly disintegrated under the impact of another whizzer from nowhere.

"You idiot!" Alimonte screamed. "Stop the car! Stop it!"

God, wasn't Parelli trying to?

He sideswiped one large tree and bounded through a thicket of shrubs, then fishtailed around with the rear end wedged against a drooping willow. Alimonte was thrown against the windshield by the terrific lashing motion, but he bounced back, viciously rubbing his forehead and muttering profanities.

The rear doors popped open and the guys back there were scrambling outside.

Nobody was saying anything.

Parelli re-started the engine and let it idle while he glanced anxiously around for an understanding of what had occurred.

Two cars were blazing, roaring fireballs—both of them punched clear off the road and completely off their wheels—and nothing alive was moving over there.

The fourth car had screeched to a swinging halt broadside into the curve and its nose now pointing back toward the gate—and, yeah, Jock Malloy had handled that real sweet; mark a point on the sheet for that wheeler!

Alimonte was still rubbing his head and cussing.

Somewhere out there a chopper cut loose, and a withering fusillade began playing spoons on Jock Malloy's wheels. Those guys back there were tumbling everywhere and shooting back—at what, Indy Parelli could not have told God himself—but they looked pretty good, like they knew what the hell they were doing, and Parelli certainly hoped so.

Nobody was saying anything, though, and that was the worst part. Guns chattering and booming, guys jumping around from tree to tree, some of them falling very quietly with blood flinging out of them.

And the boss just sat there, rubbing his head and cussing to himself.

Parelli yelled, "Boss, we better—"

But then came the biggy, and Parelli the Indianapolis Wheel ran out of ideas in mid-sentence. It even jerked Alimonte out of his stupor—a great, groaning roar followed instantly by a thunderclap that shook the air and rocked the car—and a big cloud of dust rolling out in all directions from the big joint. The whole thing was falling in, like in slow motion, like somebody had kicked out the pegs and left it nothing to stand on and it was coming unglued layer by layer.

Alimonte groaned, "He blew up the palace!"

And Parelli said, in an awed voice, "Yeah. *God!*"

Then this big tall guy in a black outfit with war stuff strung all over him came striding through the trees, a military-style automatic blowing shit all over the place. He was sweeping straight toward Parelli's beloved wheels when one of the guys from Malloy's car jumped out from behind a tree and threw down on him with both barrels from a shotgun. The tall guy danced away from that, skipping to cover behind a tree and laying back on that poor shit over there with the empty shotgun.

Indy Parelli would never apologize to anybody for what he did then. His boss was sitting there in a daze with blood seeping from a clout on his forehead. All the other guys were out there some place running

117

through the woods and firing at chiggers. And there simply was nothing left for Parelli to do.

He threw that big powerhouse into hot traction and spun the hell out of that mess, careening through the stand of timber and not exactly missing all of it all of the time but getting the hell out of there just the same, putting distance between himself and certain death—and he managed to get it back onto the road about halfway to the gate, hitting that pavement with a screech of tires and a puff of burning rubber and sending every horse he had in a dead heat for that finish line up there.

He hit the gate doing sixty—braking and spinning and tromping again to power into the turn—and he thought he was home clean until the corner of his eyes caught the looming vision of that goddamn delivery truck, going faster than any goddamn delivery truck had a right to—and there was no avoiding this one.

He spun the wheel and tromped the gas anyway, hoping for a miracle and finding nothing there but a sigh and a groan.

They came together with a horrible rending, shrieking, and grinding of metal against metal—then Parelli's mind spun out of all that, leaving it for good and all.

Wheelman Parelli had just wheeled his last mile.

At the moment, also, it appeared that perhaps a certain chief of police intelligence would ponder no more the anachronistic anomalies of military *vs.* police methods, computers and shivers, or the relativities of good and evil.

That goddamn delivery van was no goddamn *delivery* van.

16:   FEELING IT

Tom Postum possessed two minds with regard to his present circumstance. One was calm, composed, and almost detached from the whole experience—the other alarmed, worried, and contemplating a premature death.

That other vehicle was afire. He knew that. He could hear the flames and occasionally glimpse them. That being the case, there was a strong possibility that the fire would spread to his vehicle—and Tom Postum could not get out of his.

The van was lying on its side. The nose was punched in and wrapped about the lower half of his body. It was still there, that lower half, he knew that, because he could feel it and he could feel the blood soaking into his trousers legs.

There was discomfort, but no excruciating pain. So what did that mean? Was it true that "the big ones" never hurt much? Was he bleeding to death? Or would the fire get to him first? Which way did he prefer to go?

It was an academic question, a rhetorical one. Obviously, he preferred to not go, at all.

He thought of Janice and the kids, and wondered how they would take the news. Funny, he'd never thought of that before. One did not normally consider such distressing things.

"You see, honey, daddy was a stupid desk cop who just couldn't resist playing games of intrigue in the streets. So the dumb shit got into one game too many—a very clever game called Stonehenge. And that is why we are putting daddy in the ground today. Understand? Now, be sure you do your homework before we go to the funeral."

Janice had always been a great gal. Cool and calm, always cool and calm—except in bed. Would the next guy understand Janice's bedtime needs? Would he adore her as Tom Postum had adored her? And would he take care of the kids the way—

God! This was crazy!

Someone would come along! Any minute now—any second! All those explosives and gunfire. Surely someone would get involved to the extent *at least* of phoning it in.

Someone *heard it, surely*!

Sure. Sure.

And there he was.

A pair of hands were gripping that door, up there. Here I am, guy, right here, look inside, I'm down here on the damn—well, dammit, Postum's *throat* wasn't wrapped in that steel vise!

"Down here," he croaked, surprised by the reedy sound his voice made.

A head poked in up there, a rather handsome head though a bit grimy and obviously greatly fatigued. A pair of steady blue eyes glared down at him, sizing up the situation with a single glance, and a coldly familiar voice told him, "Hang tight. We'll spring you."

The head disappeared but that same voice was giving instructions to a third party. "Tool box at the rear. Get the crowbar and the torch. Guy's trapped in there."

Mack the damn guy Bolan.

How poetic.

Another voice out there, droll but a bit disturbed: "Better make it quick."

"Get the foam bottle, Gadgets. Saturate this strip of ground and try to work it around to the gas tank."

Then the guy was back at the window and lowering himself inside. He looked intently into Postum's eyes, then placed a thumb on one of them and peeled the eyelid high.

"Much pain?" that cold voice inquired—but it was not all that cold, not really—there was an undertone of, believe it or not, compassion.

"Not much," Postum said throatily. "Am I all there?"

"What I can see is." The guy was feeling of him, and reaching into intimate places. "Give me your hand." Postum did so automatically, without wondering. Bolan was positioning it, carefully but forcefully, into the inner thigh just off the groin. "Keep a pressure there. More, bear down hard. You're losing blood, and it could get worse when I start prying around down here. Hold that pressure!"

The cop assured the fugitive that he would do so.

A crowbar appeared at the window, followed closely by a dark head—Mexican, Puerto Rican, something like that. A bland voice belonged to that concerned face. "Better not risk the torch, Sarge, except as a last resort. The fumes out here are terrible."

How 'bout that? *Sarge*, was it?

Postum was surprised to hear himself saying, "Leave the crowbar and beat it. I probably have more time than you have."

The Sarge ignored that twaddle. He had the crowbar positioned across Postum's thighs, and those massive shoulders were going into a flex. "This may hurt a little. Keep that pressure."

"I said beat it, Bolan. I'm a cop."

"Do tell," the guy grunted as he lay into the bar.

"I'm Tom Postum."

The veins were popping in that neck, muscles bunched and rippling across that tired face. "Yeah, I know."

Omniscient, sure. Perhaps omnipotent, as well. That metal was creaking, giving, lifting. A rush of warmth shot along those pinned legs.

"Keep that pressure!"

Postum saw what he meant. Blood was spurting down there, now. The guy grabbed his hand and jammed it into the groin.

"Like that!"

"I guess I don't have the strength."

"Pol! I need a tourniquet!"

A length of clear plastic tubing dropped through the hole. Bolan grabbed it and applied it to the right leg, just above the knee. Then those strong hands were running along both of Postum's legs, exploring, squeezing. He turned in half profile, showing the cop a solemn smile. "No breaks, I guess. I don't hear you yelling."

The Chicano reappeared at the window. "Need me in there?"

"No room, Pol. I'm going to hand him out. Get Gadgets over here."

Almost instantly, it seemed, Postum was being lifted and dragged from the wrecked vehicle. Someone looped a dark bandage across his eyes. He wanted to tell that guy there was nothing wrong with his eyes but then it occurred to him that the bandage was for *their* benefit, not his.

A voice he'd heard quite a bit of lately on the radio quietly confirmed that. "It's okay, this is just 'til we get you inside."

122

Another voice, that hard one, commanded, "Shag it. We're into negative numbers."

Postum was carried quickly to another vehicle, a large one, to judge by the way those guys were moving him, and almost immediately they were in motion. He was deposited gently on a soft surface and that voice, distant now, again commanded, "Get me a situation, Gadgets!"

Someone was kneeling there beside him—the Chicano, probably—fiddling with the tourniquet and making deft touches farther down.

"We're on county property," reported the soft voice of "Gadgets" from nearby. Right, right, Postum was out of jurisdiction. "Scan recorders have no contacts, no reaction."

Unbelievable.

Nobody had phoned this in? *This?*

The Chicano removed the blindfold.

Postum was in a bunk. This was an RV. A bunk down the way was occupied, also. An old man, hands taped to his belly, blindfolded. What the hell *was* this?

The Chicano looked terrible. He wore combat fatigues and they were torn, dirty, blood-streaked. An angry red welt traversed his forehead an inch above the eyes—and it looked to Postum like a bullet graze. But the guy was smiling at him—wearily, but smiling.

"You had a close one," the Chicano told him.

"Don't I know it," Postum replied weakly.

That voice from up front called, "You want to come take the con, Gadgets?"

Postum saw the soft-voiced one then—a mild-looking guy with what must have been a perpetual smile. He threw a sympathetic look at Postum and went forward.

A moment later, the big guy himself was coming back. He, too, looked like hell but more so. That good face was powder-blackened and sort of scorched looking. Postum had seen the look on a battlefield or two. The left hand had been seeping blood from a welt similar to the one on the Chicano's forehead. An area the size of Postum's head was missing from the black jersey, up near the right armpit, and the flesh showing through there was raw and oozing.

Postum had never seen a man who looked so weary.

Something inside of him reacted to that, reached out to it, and his detached mind was again surprised to hear his own voice telling the guy, "You need to lay it down, man."

The big guy smiled at him and dropped into a padded chair.

Postum knew. He knew all about combat and what it did to a man. Pitched combat takes it out of any man, summoning all the vital juices to the demands of survival—and a guy had just so many of those juices. From what he'd heard of this one, this damn guy, he should have run out long ago.

But something perverse and wicked was tugging at the psyche of this cop. He realized that when he overheard himself digging the weary warrior. "I just came from your little *My Lai*."

"From my what?"

"The massacre at River Road."

"Didn't like what you saw, eh?"

"Not exactly."

The guy lit a cigarette and released the smoke on a shuddering sigh. "Well, neither did I. If you were just a bit better at your job, Postum, maybe neither of us would have to see a thing like that. You and the other cops, all of you, the hundreds of thousands of you. Why the hell aren't you doing your damn jobs?"

"You're right," Postum admitted. "It was a cheap shot. Particularly since I am here through your courtesy. Take it back."

The Chicano was attending the wounded leg.

124

Postum winced with something the guy was pouring into the gash.

The "damn guy" was staring at his cigarette. "Want a smoke, Postum?"

"Thanks, no. You're right, you know. If we cops . . ."

The guy could hardly hold himself erect. Postum wondered how long it'd been since he'd slept. A guy on the run, a guy covering his ass from both sides and still trying to strike back, a guy in *this* situation . . .

"That was 'weary' speaking, Postum. Forget it. We're all soldiers of the same side. None of us make the laws or write the rules of procedure."

That voice was fading. The guy was hurting.

"You cops aren't losing your war on the streets. You're losing it in the courts, in the city halls, in the legislatures and the congress—you're losing it to the lawyers, guy."

"You should take a strike vote," the Chicano put in with a sour smile. "Turn the thing around. No convictions, no arrests—see? Drive them all crazy. No arrests, no legal fees—see? No arrests, no clout money at city hall. No arrests, no political influence. No arrests, no damn judges at all. Who needs 'em—see?"

"I see," Postum replied, smiling weakly. "It *would* drive them up the walls, wouldn't it? It'll never happen, though."

" 'Course it won't," the Chicano or whatever replied. He stretched around to pluck the cigarette from the big guy's fingers, then dropped it into an ashtray.

Yeah—the guy was asleep. Sitting there upright—dead asleep.

The tough intelligence cop—with one or the other of his minds—had an uncomfortable desire to weep.

"I don't believe that damn guy," he quietly declared.

"Nobody does," the dark one said. "All these years I've known him, and I still don't. You're a fink, Postum, if you ever lay one finger of weight on that man's head."

"I'm a cop. I'm—"

"So what sacred damn rap is that? What's so hidebound about being a cop that you have no eyes to see and no ears to hear? We're dropping you at a hospital, guy. The Sarge says you're to have some books and stuff we 'My Lai'd' out of that shitpalace back there. We'll drop that off with you. If that's not enough for you, then you can go to hell, and I'm seceding from this damn human race."

And suddenly Postum had it—*he knew*—and the two halves of himself came together in that understanding.

"No need to do that on my account, Pol," he said weakly, but feeling stronger than he'd felt in years.

No. Not on Postum's account, Pol.

If it took a "Stonehenge" to unseal the eyes and unplug the ears, then there should be one on every street corner.

That damn guy there in the chair, that Mack the guy Bolan—*he* was the ultimate Stonehenge—a blazing anachronism from an heroic past when men could draw a firm line between right and wrong, and stand on that line—and die on that line, if necessary.

Stonehenge was ultimately revealed.

And Tom Postum felt more the man because of it. Better than that, he was more the *cop* because of it.

17:   THE GAME

Bolan awoke to the aroma of sizzling bacon and perking coffee. He was in his bunk, stripped to the shorts. A battle compress had been lightly taped over the buckshot scrape-wound on his chest.

Blancanales was bent over the bunk, dabbing at his face with a vile-smelling sponge.

"Situation," Bolan requested in a thick voice.

"You have some powder burns here, Sarge. How long since your last tetanus booster?"

"It's been awhile."

"It figures. Okay." Blancanales had worked with the medics during the early days in Vietnam. And he'd been the unofficial Able Team medic in the field. "Let's have the arm."

Damn guy was giving him a shot.

Bolan grunted and asked, "What time is it?"

The Pol withdrew the needle and lay it on a pad of gauze. "Nearly noon."

"Damn! You shouldn't have . . ."

Bolan was struggling to get upright and finding that task difficult, due to a couple hundred pounds of pressure being exerted from the other side of the struggle. "Stay put, dammit!" Blancanales commanded. "Take every minute you can! Look, Sarge, you've got to start taking better care of yourself. You don't sleep, you don't eat—how long you expect to keep it together that way?"

Bolan relented, with a grin. "The food does smell good. Is it a Schwarz production?"

"Yeah. But I guess you'll survive it. What can you do to mess up scrambled eggs and bacon?"

"I heard that," came the soft voice from the galley. "They're not scrambled. They're fluffed. See, I put in some cheese chips—that adds to the protein count—and I chopped up some little red peppers and folded them in, then I—"

"He can mess it up," the Pol said, rolling his eyes in despair.

"You don't have to eat it," Schwarz amiably replied to that.

Bolan's gaze was bouncing about the warwagon. "Looks like you've been working around me," he observed.

"Yeah. I figured to let you sleep through the routine. We dropped the cop at the hospital and turned over the stuff to him. Then we stashed Jules and went to look in on Toni."

"So?"

The Pol's face was a deadpan mask as he unfolded a sheet of lined writing paper and handed it over for Bolan's inspection. It was a crudely lettered message in spidery block print, unsigned—but there was no doubt as to the author.

"The bambina's okay as long as you don't get cute so don't worry none about that. IOU thanks but that don't mean we got a love affair here. A truce okay(?)

128

while you get out of town and leave the rest to me. We let the bambina go when you show up out of town."

Bolan bitterly commented, "Dammit."

"Sounds, uh, not too bad—for right now," Pol said.

"How long is right now?" Bolan asked him.

"Somehow I just don't feel worried about her," Pol insisted. "She can charm a puff adder. Aside from the complication of . . ."

Bolan grimaced and said, "Yeah. It's a hell of a complication, Pol."

"When are you going to let me in on the secret, Sarge?"

"These old men?"

"That's the one."

Bolan sighed and pushed himself upright. Blancanales made room and handed him a fresh shirt and slacks. Schwarz announced from the galley, "Okay, it's here if you want it."

Bolan lurched into the bathroom and carefully patted water onto his smarting face, then got into the clothing. When he emerged, the other two were seated at the mess table—Blancanales peering glumly into a cup of coffee, Schwarz carefully cutting into a large omelet.

Bolan joined them, accepted the food from Schwarz with a grateful smile, then launched into an explanation of his "game plan" as he hungrily attacked the chow.

"I haven't told you the secret because there hasn't been one," he explained. "I've just been feeling it along, playing the ear and hoping for things to fall in. I think maybe they're beginning to, now—although, Pol, I wasn't planning anything like this for Toni."

Blancanales waved his hand at that apology.

"Here's the situation—which you both know already, but let's run it past once again, anyway. This town has been a mob sleeper for a lot of years. Very quiet, no waves at all—no flamboyant personalities

129

strutting around, no national attention from congressional committees or federal strike forces, nothing. The town has been asleep."

Blancanales nodded and Schwarz said, "From the neck up, yeah. There's plenty of action down on those streets, though, Sarge."

"That's the situation," Bolan said, agreeing with Schwarz. "But look at it now. Cops prowling everywhere and harassing everyone, strike forces working their quiet games, rumbles in the congress, a ground swell of reform politics."

"Sure, Blancanales said. "Someone's disturbing the sandbox."

"Exactly. Jerry Ciglia, with a franchise from New York. St. Louis will never sleep again. Not in the same old way, at any rate. Whatever happens now, the town will never again be the same."

"Couldn't happen," Schwarz softly agreed.

"These eggs are damn good, Gadgets."

A triumphant glance went to Blancanales. "Thanks. It's the cheese and peppers."

"Cheese and peppers, okay," Pol grudgingly allowed. "Just so you don't start crediting electronic enzymes and solid-state proteins."

Bolan chuckled and continued. "I've been trying to wage a war of attrition. Well, it never worked in 'Nam—I don't know why I thought it would work here. These guys are like jacks in the box. Close the lid on one, up it pops immediately with a different jack. It's an endless game, and it's a game I'm losing. I thought maybe here—given the place and the unusual circumstances—well, I thought I'd try on a new game."

His companions exchanged glances.

Blancanales said, "We were wondering. About Artie, I mean, then Vino Jules. It, uh, it just didn't figure."

"If I can't control the lid to the box," Bolan explained quietly, "then at least maybe I can hand pick the jacks. Follow?"

A grin spread across Schwarz's face.

Blancanales said, "Artie and Jules are more acceptable jacks than Ciglia and Annunzio."

"That's the idea," Bolan said. "They're old, semi-retired, running a few quiet games here and there, nothing big—they're more like fleas on the lamb's back, not wolves waiting to devour the whole animal."

"You couldn't play a game like that just anywhere," Blancanales decided.

"No, I couldn't. And maybe it won't work here, even. But I think it's worth a try. Look—the territory will always be here. Once established, it never dies out completely. I could come back here once a month and whack everything in sight, and every month there'd be new heads to whack. So let's suppose that I whack Artie, I whack Jules, and the whole cadre. Then I turn to Ciglia and I whack him and his cadre. And when I fade over the horizon to the next battleground, there's a vacuum here in St. Louis that's going to suck a whole new regime into the box. There'll be another Ciglia— and, after him, another one—and on and on."

"Frustrating, isn't it," Schwarz said with a droll smile.

"Worse than that," Bolan said. "These young turks are like a pack of ravenous wolves. Give them a territory and they start ripping through it and devouring everything in their paths."

"Won't New York just send someone down to continue the penetration if you take out Ciglia and leave Artie?" Schwarz asked.

"Depends on how well I stack Artie's box," Bolan replied. "It's a delicate game and I'm not sure I can work it. But I'm going to try. When I leave this town, I hope to leave the locals in firm control—from the mob standpoint, that is. I want Little Artie to stand up and

131

thumb his nose at New York—maybe even shake his withered old fist in their gluttonous faces—and *dare* them to by God send him another Jerry Ciglia."

"I get the lay," Blancanales said grimly.

"You want Artie to get the credit for beating Ciglia," Schwarz decided.

"That's about it," Bolan said. "Now, *compadres*—how the hell do I go about doing that?"

"You stack the deck, I guess," Blancanales said thoughtfully.

"The box, not the deck," Schwarz corrected him.

"But then there's Toni," Bolan said with a sigh.

Silence enveloped the table.

Presently, Blancanales released a long sigh and said, "We just have to spring her first, that's all."

"Where's the spring?" Bolan inquired.

"Right here."

Bolan nodded. "Okay. Use whatever it takes, but find her. You guys know the local scene much better than I do, so that part of the game is yours. Gadgets, I'll need a car."

"It's parked right outside," Schwarz said, grinning. "Bought and paid for, courtesy of the Stonehenge branch of the Mafia International Bank. And I already got it wired."

Bolan grinned back. "Okay. I have a date at the airport. I'll check back with you in exactly two hours."

He was strapping himself into the Beretta quiet leather. Schwarz tossed him a jacket.

Blancanales said, "We'll start with a pick-up pass of the standard drops. Could be something interesting on those recorders."

Bolan nodded his agreement with that idea, then gave the guy a close look. "How's the head?" he asked him.

Pol brushed the forehead welt with the back of his

132

hand. "That's a humility reminder," he replied with a sour smile. "It's a plus, not a minus."

Bolan went out of there smiling soberly. Pluses and minuses—that was what it all came down to in the final accounting. Would St. Louis end up as a plus or a minus?

He did not have the answer to that. The answer lay somewhere *out there*, on those streets and in the minds of desperate men who well understood the desperate games of survival in a hostile world.

For now, Bolan had to take time out from that world to address a personal problem in the other one. He hoped that the problem would turn out to be a minor one. There simply was no room for any other kind— not at this stage of the St. Louis game. He sighed and sent the new vehicle cruising to a rendezvous with the world of Eden. "Johnny, Johnny," he muttered. "If only I could tell you what a beautiful world it is."

18: THE DECISION

Leo Turrin had been balancing on the sharp edge of a knife for many years, and he'd lately taken to wondering how much longer his nervous system would tolerate the strain. His marriage was feeling it, that much was certain. He'd managed to keep Angelina ignorant of even his mob activities for longer than one might expect—due, probably, to the fact that Angie was simply that sort of woman. She accepted things on faith and didn't get too nosy about her husband's business affairs. At one time, that is.

Bolan the Bold had changed all that, and in a highly distressing manner. The guy had come gunning for him—and Leo Turrin still could not think about that unsettling bit of business without feeling the chills up his spine all over again.

Miracle of miracles, Angie had been the one to save him from that. Of all the people in the world who might take up a gun and begin popping away at somebody—his Angelina had gone gunning for Mack Bolan!

Odd, sometimes, how things work—the funny, kinky turns that life can take to ravel a guy up and keep him keeping on. Probably nothing Leo could have said or done would have saved his blood from Bolan's grim reaper effect on that chilling night when the big guy came to collect.

Face it, Leo was no match in warfare to a guy like Bolan. Who, after all, was?

And it had been his misfortune to be the selfsame "Leo" whom Bolan had been taking Pittsfield apart to find. No badge and no credentials would have stopped that guy at that time and place.

But Angelina had stopped him.

And she'd done it with a twenty-five-calibre pop gun—emptied the clip at the guy and even connected with a lucky shot. Leo had never asked Bolan about that night—had never inquired why he hadn't simply disarmed Angelina and gone on with the grim business at hand instead of turning around. Certainly the guy had stood up many times to far more formidable threats than a hysterical woman with a pop gun.

It had to do, Turrin suspected, with the size of the inner man, himself. Bolan was as large inside as outside. Something inside—not fear but something far more moving, more commanding than fear—had responded to that little woman's determination to keep her husband alive. Compassion, maybe. It was a word that could lose a lot of meaning in this confusing age, but Leo Turrin believed that he understood true compassion and he believed that he at least partially understood the inner man that was Mack Bolan.

Anyway, Angelina then knew about the mob angle. She'd not been able to live with that, not without all of it, so he'd had to tell her also about his federal commission—and Turrin's life had been growing more and more complicated ever since.

Bolan had the right idea, probably. You could not

136

mix the two worlds together and make the thing jell properly. You ended up weaker in each, less effective in both.

But, *God*, Leo's life would not be worth living without Angelina and the kids. That was one of the principal differences between himself and Bolan. Bolan could go it alone, and he could find reasons for even wishing to do so. Leo Turrin could not. And he had no apologies for that weakness. It was not, he knew, in the final sum of things, a weakness at all. It was simply a difference.

But he'd always been in awe of Mack Bolan.

The kid brother was, also.

Johnny had been on pins and needles throughout that long flight from Pittsfield. Thrilled and scared all at once. Thrilled to be going, to be seeing his brother again. Scared of what he might find at the end of that flight—of the reception he might receive. Scared of being thought silly and immature, of being judged harshly for a rash act. Scared most of all, probably, of being totally rejected by the man he'd come to regard as something of a God.

The kid hardly knew his brother, when you got right down to it. Hero worship, sure—but that's not *knowing*, it's not understanding the inner works of a man. After all, Mack had gone to the army while Johnny was a toddler. The trips home had been rare and brief—although usually, according to Johnny, the two had always spent a lot of time together when the sarge did come home.

And, then, of course, there'd been that final homecoming. What a horror, what a miserable damn ...

It was another memory that never failed to chill Leo Turrin. Because, in God's sight, Leo Turrin had been partially responsible for that tragedy. No badge could shield him from that.

And it was no mere accident that Mack Bolan had

gone a-gunning for Leo. It was, correspondingly, no mere accident that Leo Turrin had taken personal responsibility for the well-being of this kid brother—for as long as Leo might go on living.

And now the kid did have a genuine problem—in his own mind, anyway. Leo did not begrudge him this time to help straighten out that problem. Not that the resolution was going to turn the way Johnny was hoping for. No way. No way whatever. And Leo could only hope that the sarge would have the time and frame of mind to handle the thing properly.

It was a tender age, Johnny's was. It was the age when it was so terribly easy to go haywire.

And, yeah, Leo Turrin hoped . . .

The kid had brought all that damn luggage—imagine!—just to go around the block on an airplane—two damn heavy suitcases, and he insisted on dragging them along all by himself.

Leo finally convinced him to give them to a porter—hey, the guy has to make a living, kid, give him the bags!

The porter had just taken the tip and dropped the suitcases at the motel jitney stand outside the terminal when this blue car pulled up and the tall guy in the denim suit and dark glasses stepped out and called over to Leo.

"Leo! Your car."

He hadn't recognized that figure right off, but there was no mistaking that voice.

Johnny looked like he was about to pass out.

The guy grinned at him and got into the back of the car. Leo tossed the bags in front and ran around to get behind the wheel.

"Let's go, let's go," he called to the boy.

Johnny shyly slid in beside the big guy and offered him a hand.

138

Bolan went right past that hand, swept the dark glasses away, and wrapped the kid in a bear hug.

Leo's eyes were damp as he wheeled out of there. A reunion like that did not occur every day in the life of Leo Turrin—and this one, very likely, would prove to be the final one for these two.

Bolan stepped over to the window, lit a cigarette, and gazed down onto the pool area as he quietly requested, "Give me that again now, John?"

"I said . . ." I think . . . I'm old enough, now . . . we should be together."

"You mean . . ." Bolan waved a hand. "All the time, permanent, a pair."

"Yeah. We're the only Bolans left. We belong together."

"We've been through this a couple of times," Bolan reminded him.

"I know, but—I've grown some since then. I've been thinking it over. Both of us . . . alone . . . this way. Why shouldn't we be together?"

"John, that would be the greatest thing. I can't think of anything I'd rather—but it can't be. You know why. I thought the older you got, the better you'd understand that."

The kid's eyes wavered and fell. He was fighting a hopeless battle, and he seemed to know it. "Leo told me about your bus—your RV. It sounds neat. I figured we could, sort of, like *live* in it, you know. I could wheel it for you, Mack. I'm a good driver. An hour or two, you could show me, I could handle that bus fine. I could even do the cooking, stuff like that. Leo says you don't eat right. I could remind you. I got a cookbook in my suitcase. Tells you how to fix all sorts of nourishing meals."

Bolan was genuinely touched. He turned back to the window as he said, "You ready to start housewifing it,

139

John? Know what you'd have to give up for that? What about school? Your friends, your studies, the proms and pep rallies and all the fun things, organized sports, girls—especially that." He flashed a look from the shoulder. "You have a girl?"

The kid nodded his head.

"Pretty close thing, is it?"

"Well, yeah, I guess so."

"You ready to tell her goodbye?"

"I already did."

Turrin nervously lit a cigar. When was the kid going to get around to the main event?

Bolan was telling him, "I live in the hellgrounds, John. You can't imagine what that's like, no matter how old you are, until you've lived there awhile. It's a lousy life. It's no life at all. It's a sort of a death, John. You trust no one, talk to no one, believing nothing. Every man, woman, and boy you meet you have to see as a possible enemy, someone who'd trade your head for a few bucks. There are no hands of friendship, no community of minds—there's nothing but the hellgrounds. And you're ready to trade what you have for that?"

"You did," Johnny replied stubbornly.

"What am I?" Bolan shot back, half-angrily. "Look at me, John. Look! What the hell am I? Is this something to copy?"

"I'd follow you to hell," the kid said between gritted teeth.

"You already did!" Bolan spat back. "And I told you that you should never do this! I thought you understood!"

Easy, easy. Turrin wanted to say.

"Mack I—I had to. I had no choice."

Here it comes. The main event.

"There's always a choice between heaven and hell, John."

The big guy's eyes were moist, the emotions tightly reined again but peeping out through those eyes.

"I made my choice out at that cemetery behind St. Agnes. You helped me make it. I'm keeping my end. I expect you to keep yours."

"I choose hell, too!" The kid was hanging in there. The "main event" had not yet arrived.

Bolan was all but groaning as he replied, "Johnny! There'd be no sense to *hell* if there were no *people* in *heaven*! I want some of *mine* there! *One*, anyway!"

Oh God! Turrin wished he'd excused himself and disappeared for awhile—and now it was too late.

Johnny had finally arrived at it.

"That, uh, brings up—Mack, I told you I had no choice. Val, uh, she, uh . . ."

"What about her?"

"She's getting *married*, dammit!"

The big guy just stood there for a frozen moment, framed in that window with the sun's rays streaming in behind him. Very quietly, then, he said, "It's about time, isn't it? It's what I want, John. Hey—Val owes not a damn thing to either of us. She deserves—"

"I didn't say she did!"

"Who's the lucky guy?"

"A G-man." Pained eyes flicked to Turrin. "One of his."

"You like him?"

"I guess he's okay. Val thinks he is. That makes it okay by me. How about you?"

"I'm with you," the elder Bolan said.

"Well, you see, that's why—I mean, it's time now you and I hooked up. That's what I thought."

No one should ever try to tell Leo Turrin that Mack Bolan was anything but 100 percent human being. Leo knew how much Val meant to that guy. He *knew*. He'd been there when the guy was running wild through Boston, smashing that town to splinters in the frenzied

141

search for her, one dismal night. Leo had been there, too, when the guy sprung her from a fate worse than several deaths and then told her goodbye, finally, with no open doorways anywhere that would allow a repetition of the Boston thing. Turrin had personally overheard that emotional and tearful parting. Bolan had made the agonizing decision, and he'd given her back to the world—to the *bright* world. Even so—even though Leo knew of a certainty that this was precisely what Bolan had wanted for her for so long—even so, this thing now had to be like a hot knife in an old wound. The hurt could find no surface of that chiseled face to torment—but it was there in the eyes, that final misery was there, and Leo Turrin knew it.

"It's going to be hard on you for awhile, John," the big guy was telling the kid brother. "Sure, you're going to miss her. But you have to think of it—you need to realize that Val is a human being, a very warm and giving human being, and she has needs. She can't spend the rest of her life—"

"Mack, dammit!" the kid yelled.

"There's more?"

There's plenty more, Turrin silently assured him.

"There's a hook in it," the kid said quietly.

"What's the hook?"

"She won't leave *me*."

"What do you mean?"

"It's a—a condition. She says either I go with her ... or she doesn't go."

A terrible thing was occurring upon Mack Bolan's face. Turrin got up and went to the bathroom to wash his hands.

"You'd better lay it out for me, John."

"Well, Jack—that's the guy, Jack Gray—he says he's marryin' *both* of us. Isn't that a hell of a kick? They want to *adopt* me, Mack. The whole trip. Change

142

my name and everything. Move away somewhere. *Change my name.*"

Bolan caught Leo Turrin's eye through the open door. There was a question there, and Turrin returned a silent answer.

"What's wrong with that?" Bolan quietly asked the kid. "You've got an assumed one now. I have a hundred or so."

"Well, sure, but that's temporary."

"John—do you realize—do you truly understand what Val is doing? I mean, what she's—"

"She means well," the kid said.

"Means well? You're telling me she has a chance to live a normal life with a good man?—that she won't go unless you're in the package?—and she just *means* well?"

"Mack—I—we'd *both* be deserting you. I can't do that."

Turrin returned to his chair and dropped into it with a sigh. Storm signals were flying in the Bolan gaze—in *both* Bolan gazes.

"Let's understand something, John. You and I can always be together in spirit, and I sure hope we will. But that's the only way."

"That's a lot of bull, Mack! I could be a second gun for you. I could be—"

There it went down.

Turrin kept waiting for the other shoe to fall, but there was only a suffocating silence.

You blew it, kid. You said the one thing you could never say. And the kid knew it. He ran out of gas in the shadow of that towering horror spilling from that big grim man at the window—and the battle was over, right there.

"Time for plain talk, John."

"Okay," the kid replied, very quietly, very subdued.

"You can't come with me because I can't afford you.

143

You'd be a noose around my neck. You'd be my death, John. I wouldn't live long enough for you to get the feel of a gun."

"I—I can't do the other."

"Why not?"

"I can't desert you. Not while you're . . ."

"Not while I'm living—right? What are you doing, John, laying the death watch on me?"

"I—I can't desert you."

"Why not? I deserted you."

"That's different."

"Wish me well, John. And tell me goodbye. Then go wish Val well. And tell her thanks."

The kid was crying, and they were painful tears— tears of defeat, of helpless rage, of shame at the tears themselves.

Leo returned to the bathroom and flushed the toilet, then decided to wash his face.

When he returned to the room, things were pretty much as when he'd left—the sarge at the window, scowling—the kid sitting there with acid tears streaming down his face and blinding him, gnawing holes in his bottom lip.

"It's a bum rap, John," Bolan was saying quietly. "We just have to make the best of it, and go on. Tell you what. This is no way to say goodbye. You hang in here at the motel for a while. Give me another day with this town. If I haven't returned by this time tomorrow, it's because I won't be returning. You go back with Leo. But if I can make it back—if I do—we'll return to Pittsfield together. We'll take it slow, and enjoy it. You can drive the bus and take all the galley duty you can stomach. We'll make a week of it—a week to remember. And when we get there, John, you'll go your way and I'll go mine—without goodbye. Okay?"

"Okay," the kid said, smiling through those tears.

"I have some business to talk with Leo."

144

Bolan went over and embraced the kid, shot Turrin a tortured look, and hurried from the room.

"Back in a minute, Brother John," Turrin promised the younger Bolan as he followed the older one outside.

Some tragedies just went on and on. The one at Pittsfield had never ended. What was it the big guy had said to the kid?

Hell makes no sense if there are no people in heaven?

Turrin had to agree with that logic.

But, then, what the hell—the logic worked just as well the other way around.

And Leo Turrin, the knife-edge expert, thought he knew why some men chose hell.

19:   TO MAKE A KING

They stood stiffly in the hallway, side by side, backs to the wall, neither looking directly at the other, conversing in monotones.

"I'm trying to play kingmaker, Leo, and I can't find a handle. Give me one."

"Who do you want to crown?"

"Little Artie."

"Poor choice. I hear he's dead."

"When do you hear this?"

"This morning, coming through LaGuardia. Bit of a layover there. Spent a few dimes to pump the well. Something else, too. About a dozen head crews are under hot dispatch to this town."

"So what's new?"

"The priority. You happen to be an incidental this time. They're coming to sweep this town of the deadwood."

"That's Cosa Nostra for you, Leo. That's real brotherhood."

"When you're hot you're hot, Sarge. And when you're not . . ."

"Artie's not dead. He's alive and spitting."

"You have that for a fact?"

"Yeah."

"Good for him. The last of a line, Sarge. A true don, a real Godfather image."

"Bull."

Turrin chuckled. "With all that means, of course."

"Where should I look for him?"

"Ciglia's the one to be looking for. He's the one with the crown, now."

"It makes no difference that Artie is still around?"

"Not in the end, no. I told you, the cleansing wind is blowing."

"What if Artie could turn that wind around? What if he could spit clear to New York on that turnaround?"

"Like I said, when you're hot you're hot. Sure. The wiseguys would have to rethink their position."

"That's my game, Leo."

"Oh. Well. I don't know, Sarge. Kingmaker, eh? Okay, maybe. It would take a lot of finesse."

"Give me a handle, Leo."

"They're saying in New York that you whacked Little Artie."

"No. Ciglia had him locked up. I sprung him. But I couldn't hang on. He's on the loose, with all of Ciglia's professional guns hunting him down. Also, the old man took off with something I treasure greatly, something fragile. Where do I start looking?"

"Hmmmm."

"Leo?"

"I'm thinking about it. Is old man Pattriccia still around?"

"As of a couple hours ago, yes."

"He's an old river rat, you know. Peddled booze along the Mississippi all during prohibition. Some years back, he—aw no, that's too far back. I heard nothing more about it."

"What is it? A straw, Leo—any straw."

"I think . . . if Artie is in trouble, he'd try to hole up with Vino Jules. They go way back together."

"What about that straw?"

"It's not a straw, it's a boat. A genuine, authentic, museum piece of a boat. Old stern-wheeler. It was headed for the graveyard and Jules picked it up as a sentimental—I don't know, Sarge, it was just a ghost thought. I've heard nothing about that boat for years. The old man was going to restore it and keep it as a plaything, I guess. Relive his youth, retire to the river, something like that. He never did it, Sarge. But I remember there was a write-up in some national magazine—a sort of nostalgia thing—when Jules rescued the old hulk. Pictures and everything. It was, uh, yeah—the *Jubilee*—the SS *Jubilee*. Big, three-decker—I don't know, probably carry several hundred people. Cruise boat, you know. These rivers used to be full of them."

"I know the kind," Bolan said. "There are still a few around. Couple tied up at the foot of town right now."

"Right. That would be, uh, probably—what's the name of that showboat?—the *Golden*—the *Goldenrod*. Sits here all the time. Then there's that streamliner—the, uh, *President* or the *Admiral* or something. Both of those outclass the *Jubilee* by a couple of light-years, though. Like I said, the thing was falling apart. The magazine story gave Jules a lot of embarrassment. Got to be a big joke up east. Jules got the old scow for scrapper's prices but it was going to take—I don't know—a ridiculous lot of bucks to restore it. Everybody was laughing about it, and I think the old guy just dropped the whole project."

"You don't believe he restored it?"

"Damned if I know, Sarge. I just don't know. But it was a thought."

"Is that the only damn thing you have for me, Leo?"

"Sorry, Sarge. This place has been the end of the earth, mob-wise, for a long time. I just don't know what to tell you."

"Uh . . . this guy Jack Gray. Okay guy?"

"Damned okay guy. He's leaving the service, setting up a law office out west—Wyoming, I believe. Val and Johnny could not be better off. And it's the most perfect cover I could imagine. Jack will take care of them, Sarge."

"You know the guy personally?"

"Sure. I hand-picked him for the security job. I'll have a life-history file in your hands within a few days. Check 'im out, satisfy yourself all the way. Then send me the signal. I'll handle it."

"Leo, I don't know how to say—"

"Don't try, then. Beat it, fugitive. I gotta go see a kid that just became a man. Stay hard, guy."

They shook hands warmly and Bolan went out of there.

His head was aching with the things tumbling through it and his heart was heavy from that unsettling session with Johnny. Where Val had been was simply a numbness, now, and he did not wish to disturb that novocaine job. A hellstorm day lay ahead of him; it was here that his energies and his emotions had to go.

So . . .

The *Jubilee*, eh?

Wouldn't it be a kick if that old stern-wheeler was still around somewhere quiet?

And wouldn't it be an even bigger kick if that was where the Giamba family had been holing up lately!

If so, then maybe after all Vino Jules would have the last laugh on the wiseguys up east.

Schwarz was the one to pick up on the mobile phone. Bolan sent him rolling to a pay station for the

150

sensitive conversation which was to follow, and when the secure connection was made, Bolan asked him, "What's your situation?"

"Lousy," was the glum reply. "It's as quiet as a transistor's hiss in this town, Sarge. Feels to me like the calm before a storm."

"Not a whisper of Toni?"

"Not a one."

"I have a possible angle, Gadgets. Worth checking out, anyway. Is Jules still in our bag?"

"He's there. Cussing and ranting into my babysitter monitor."

"We need a showdown talk with that old man. You guys go over there and lay it out for him. Make him believe you. If we don't find Artie and what's left of his cadre within the next few hours, then there'll be no tomorrow for the Giamba Family. Make him understand that. Once you get his full attention, ask him about the *Jubilee*."

"What is that, Sarge?"

"It's an old river stern-wheeler he picked off the scrap heap some years back. The story at the time was that he meant to fix it up and save it for his retirement. If that boat is still around, Gadgets, stashed somewhere, it would make a beautiful hideout in times of heat. Like now."

"Yeah. That sounds better than anything I've heard. We just lay it on him, huh?"

"Finesse it a bit, Gadge. You know how. Don't rely on his good heart and cooperative spirit. Just sort of drop the name on him, like you'd picked it off a Ciglia contact or something equally disturbing. If the boat *is* our paydirt, you should get a reaction. Lay it on heavy, then. Scare hell out of him. And if you locate the boat—well, hell, I hate to even suggest this next, Gadgets."

"May as well. I'm probably ahead of you. You want us to go in there and snatch Toni—right?"

Bolan sighed. "I think you should try the soft way. It seems we already have a halfway receptive ear in the Giamba camp. If it was me, I'd walk right in there. I'd lay it out. It's life or death for them, Gadgets. There's a couple hundred hot guns converging on this town, and they're coming for Giamba blood. Now—if *we* found Artie, they will, too—eventually. He has to be made to understand that. If you can get the old man's ear, then you tell him exactly what I have in mind. I believe the idea just might appeal to him. I think he'd go for it. But he has to turn over Toni, first."

"Uh, just what *do* you have in mind, Sarge?"

"An Able special—Cong High."

"Aha. Okay. How are you going to, uh, set it up?"

"I don't know yet. I'll work something. Meanwhile, you work the old man."

"Uh, how'd your personal thing work out?"

"It's okay, Gadgets."

"Glad to hear that. Okay. If we can't get past old Jules, we'll try another route. Where the hell could you hide a boat like that? I guess it's fairly large, huh? Sort of like the *Goldenrod*?"

"So I understand, yeah. Uh, that scrapyard we hit up there today. What was on the other side of that joint?"

"The river. Well—a lot of junk first. And an old boatyard that got left high and dry when they put the levee in. Some barge docks. Mostly, though, just your general run-of-the-mill riverside, Sarge."

"There might be a tie-in somewhere there. You could check it out. Junk cars, junk boats, a salvage business. That's where I'd start looking."

"So would I. Keep yourself wired in, Sarge. I'm getting the feeling."

Bolan chuckled grimly. "Something feeding into your pre-amps, eh?"

Schwarz laughed delightedly. "Yeah, you got it."

"*You* got it, compadre," Bolan told him. "The dirty side, I'm afraid. Tell Pol I said—"

"I'll tell him you said quit goofing off and get his damn pre-amps tuned."

Bolan laughed and hung up.

There really was not much to laugh about . . . but, hell, it beat crying. And the Man from Grim had an almost tearful task to contemplate.

He had to get Jerry Ciglia's ear.

In a most commanding manner.

Bolan had to get the St. Louis Hots lined into a Cong High kill.

And he did not know, at that very moment, just how the hell he was going to accomplish that.

20:   THE CONG HIGH LURE

Ciglia was huddled with several of the newly arrived crew bosses, in the library of the Giamba mansion, when Tony Bird, the yard chief, brought him the Ace of Spades business card with the name Billy Kingdom engraved in silver on the back.

It produced an impressed silence at the conference table.

"Who's this guy?" Ciglia asked, frowning at the card.

"I got him holding at the gate, boss. He says I should shake my ass, he ain't sitting out there all day."

"You boys heard of Billy Kingdom?" the Lord of St. Louis asked his visitors.

"Those guys got a thousand names," one growled.

"And a thousand faces," said another.

"I know another guy with a thousand names and faces, though," Ciglia worriedly told them.

The gunner from Cincinnati snickered. "Don't think he would be checking in *here*, do you, Jerry?"

Ciglia was chewing his lip. "You never know."

A respectful silence ruled that assembly as the visitors exchanged knowing looks. Hot-Ass Ciglia, those looks said, had the rattles. It was understandable, of course, considering all that had gone down in this town the past few hours.

The yard boss fidgeted in the background for a moment, then said, "What do I tell 'im, boss? I can't leave a Black Ace sitting there at the damn gate like a—"

"Shut up, dammit!"

"Yessir."

"I want a vote from you, Tony, I'll ask you for it!"

"Sure, boss. I just thought—"

"What's this guy look like?"

The yardman shrugged. "What do they all look like?"

"What kind of answer is that!" Ciglia snarled.

"It's the only one I got, boss. He looks like all of them look."

"Well what did he say he wants?"

"He just says I should bring the card to my chairman of the board."

A light flared in those worried eyes. "He said that?"

"That's exactly it."

The "chairman of the board" of the new St. Louis corporation carefully pushed his chair back and reached for his cane. All things considered, it was fitting and appropriate that he check this guy through, himself. One did not leave an official *commissione* troubleshooter chafing in the street—not even in troubled times—*especially* not in troubled times. On the other hand, that Bolan bastard had been known to pull wild stunts at crazy times. He had even impersonated one of these *commissione* "black aces" in Ciglia's Gulf Coast field headquarters during the New Orleans rumble. Once burnt, dammit, was twice shy of the fire. It did not seem too likely that the guy would push his luck with another try at the same gambit with the same

156

pigeon, though. The guy was just too intelligent to try that. Just the same . . . call it super-cautious or whatever the hell you liked, Ciglia was not leaving a judgment like this to any dumb-ass yardbirds.

His bodyguards, Jake Rio and Nate Palmieri, leapt to assist him to his feet. Rio handed him the cane and tried to manhandle him out of the chair. Putting on a show, no doubt, for the visiting ginks. Ciglia pushed the tagmen out of the way and hobbled out of there with a soft apology to the ginks for the interruption.

"Get comfortable for a minute," he told them. "I better look at this black ace for myself."

The tagmen followed him out and fell into step close behind. It was slow going, dammit. The ankle was swollen to twice the normal size and the lightest weight he put on there hurt like hell. A damned sprained ankle didn't make for a stretcher case, though. Little thing like that didn't keep a man from doing for himself. He grinned inwardly. Certainly not a chairman of the board, for chrissakes.

Nobody had ever called him that before.

It sounded good. What the hell, Jerry Ciglia was no jerk. So, okay, maybe *he* was showing off a little bit, too. Any guy with a bit of self-respect liked to do that sometimes. It was a matter of class, sometimes—having it or not having it—and Ciglia had always respected a show of true class in a guy.

What the hell, it wouldn't hurt for the old men up east to be told that the new chairman of the board of the new St. Louis subsidiary had personally come out to the gate—during a troubled and dangerous time—to greet their emissary, even with his ankle swollen up like a football.

That was class.

And if that guy out there at the gate was *not* a legit black ace . . . well, by God, *this* chairman was ably equipped to handle that sort of situation, too. With *two* swollen ankles.

Ciglia tossed a glance over his shoulder to make sure the tagmen were close behind; this rattled "chairman" was not all *that* damned sure of himself. And he was mentally spotting his boys in the yard force—Tony Bird walking ahead, others standing around at obscure posts in tense attitudes of watchfulness—with the meanest pair on the gate watch itself.

The entire force was up hard now, and it was about damn time. Ciglia had jerked around some assignments, promoting some and demoting others—creating a couple of *new* crews, even—and he'd whipped this damn force into shape damned quick.

No fancy-ass dude was going to come lightly tripping across Jerry Ciglia's turf ever again. No way, sir.

The gate, made of heavy iron pickets, probably weighed a couple of tons counting the anchor posts and the heavy lock bars. There'd be no crashing through there. It would take a tank to bust through that gate, and a company of infantry to shoot their way through it.

Ciglia was not really concerned about his base security.

He *was* concerned about his status, his franchise, and his future—considering the dumb damned things that had been done in this territory today.

Yes, it was entirely appropriate that he check out this Black Ace for himself.

The hotshot was driving a fire-red Corvette—a shiny new convertible with the top down—classy as hell with those fat whitewalls and the chrome luggage carrier on the rear deck. Some damn great-looking luggage, too.

Pure class, these boys, and didn't they know how to show it.

This one was wearing one of those classy looking checkered open-road caps and a red silk scarf to match

158

the car. Standard steel-rimmed smoked glasses. A miniature cigar with a built-on mouthpiece, angling from the side of his mouth.

A real classy guy, yeah.

And he had that "mean pair" of gatemen completely enthralled, standing there with their arms crossed and looking at the guy like he was God himself, chuckling at something the hotshot was telling them. The gate was cracked open and both of the boys were standing out there beside that hot car—and there was a violation, right there. Ciglia would crack some asses over this, exalted visitor or no. That could wait, though, for a better time.

The chairman of the board gave the gate a push with his cane and hobbled on through, pretending to scrutinize the "business card" which had been brought to him by Tony Bird.

Palmieri and Rio held up just inside the gate. Tony Bird stepped through just behind the boss and tried to catch the eyes of his errant gatemen.

The guy in the hot little car was saying ". . . all the way from Rolla. I swear. I finally stopped at this little roadside winery at St. Clair, and a minute or two later the guy pulls up behind me. I turn around and give him this, see, with the cigar, and I say, 'Morning, officer. Glorious day for a dash through the countryside, what?' "

The gatemen were breaking up.

"So the cop says, 'You were dashing at a hundred and forty miles an hour there, sir. Don't you think that's a bit much?'

"I give him the cigar bit again, and I tell him, 'For this automobile, officer? Not at all, not at all. Why, the little dear was just—'"

The "black ace" had become aware of Ciglia's presence. He broke off the recital in mid-sentence, tilted his head just a bit to the left, held up a crooked finger, and beckoned to the man with the cane to come forward.

Ciglia could not see those eyes behind the smoked lenses but he could feel the guy's gaze raking him up and down.

"Who is this?" the hotshot asked, in that same amiable tone.

Ciglia stepped closer to hand him the card. "You sent this in to me, I believe," he said, playing it cold and unsmiling. "If you're wondering about the cane, I turned my ankle this morning and that's why it took me so long to get out here and greet you personally."

"Keep it," the black ace said grandly, waving the card back. "Press it in your book of memories."

What was this *shit*!

Nobody talked to—!

Ciglia opened his mouth in a snarl to punch something back to the guy—black ace or no—and that was precisely when it happened.

No one, it was said, had ever moved so quickly. Nothing had ever changed so fast. Never had a moment of relaxed camaraderie plummeted so suddenly into a moment of such deep and ghastly desperation.

Those men present who would later be called upon by their peers to recall and relate the experience over and over again would remain steadfastly unanimous concerning the details of that shattering moment.

One instant the great man—the all-right guy—had been sitting there pleasantly jawing with the troops and entertaining them tremendously, pausing for a bantering moment with the boss. One lightning move later, the boss himself was turned around and bent backwards halfway into that little car. The snout of an ugly black pistol was jammed into his mouth—Billy Kingdom's other hand full of the boss's hair. And the thing simply froze everybody.

And "Billy Kingdom"—with a whole new voice,

now—was coldly instructing everybody on how they should go about keeping their boss alive.

"Easy, boys, easy. This trigger has a two-pound pull. All I do is breathe too hard or twitch with an itch, and your boss says goodbye to his head. I'm here to parley, and that's all I'm here for. So everybody go back inside. Lock the gate, Jake, when they're all in. Then everybody should disappear for a few minutes while Jerry and I have our talk. When that's done, Jerry goes in and I roll away. Simple as that, that's the way it can be. Of course, it could go different. Depends on you boys."

That cold speech was followed by a moment of building suspense until Palmieri assumed the responsibilities of command. The big bodyguard stood stiffly at the gate, arms spread, fingers splayed. "Everybody be cool, like the man says. Who are you really, mister?"

"The name is Bolan."

The moment became even more electric.

Jake Rio's sober tones joined the command structure. "He keeps what he says, Nate. If he says it's a parley, then it's a parley."

Palmieri could hardly bear the situation, though. There was hot anxiety in those eyes as his gaze lingered on the tortured position of his boss.

"Okay," he said, finally. "You boys get it in here. Do exactly like he says. Jerry—there's no other way. We're doing the only thing we can do."

The boys went inside.

Jake Rio locked the gate.

Everybody disappeared, but not the supercharged atmosphere.

Ciglia was bleeding from the corner of his mouth. Bolan eased the Beretta out but left the muzzle resting on the chairman's chin. He let off a little on the backbend, allowing the guy some breathing space, and icily told him, "Looks like it's just you and me, Jerry."

161

Those eyes of the chairman were cold in their terror, speculative in their desire to go on living. But Jerry Ciglia was a pretty tough guy, all things considered. "What do you want?" he mumbled.

"We can make this quick and clean. Just give me one word."

There was no posturing, no silly bravado. The chairman of the board could be a very reasonable man—with a blaster at his chin.

"Which word?"

"The name of the boat."

"What boat?"

"I said quick and clean, guy—not twenty questions."

"I don't know what the hell you want."

"I want Toni."

"Oh? Well. Didn't know you knew her. I mean, I figured she left with you, this morning, but I couldn't figure why."

"Private eye."

"Toni?"

"Yeah."

"Don't shit me, guy."

"Go to hell. I just want the name of Pattriccia's boat."

The chairman was probably a lousy poker man. He could not keep his mind out of his eyes. "Oh," he said. "Which one?"

"That old stern-wheeler everyone was laughing about."

"The *Mississippi Queen*."

"That's it?"

"You said stern-wheeler. That's the one."

"Where does he keep it?"

The chairman was not terribly inventive, either. "Out on the river somewhere."

"I didn't think maybe he kept it out on the *desert* somewhere, guy. It's a big river."

162

"I don't know where he keeps it."

"Come on, now. You've never even *seen* it?"

Those eyes were flickering, the mind tumbling. "No. No. I just heard the guys laughing about it once. I haven't been here long, you know."

"*Mississippi Queen.* You're sure."

"Oh yeah. I'm sure about that."

"I take a parley seriously, guy. I get upset with bum words. I usually come back from those. I come back feeling bad. I can get to you, Ciglia. Anywhere."

"I believe you. I'm not shitting you. It's the *Mississippi Queen.* Stern-wheeler. That's the one."

Bolan disarmed the guy, shoved him clear, and powered out of there in reverse, onto the street and clear to the corner—then ripped out with a squeal and a roar.

Neither shot nor vehicle followed, and Bolan had not really expected any.

He'd given the new "chairman of the board" something very intriguing to ponder, something to override and perhaps even compensate for that hateful and degrading experience in the driveway.

And Bolan grinned. The *Mississippi Queen*, indeed!

Ciglia had obviously never heard of Jules' folly.

But he'd sure gone down quick for the Cong High lure.

21:   PATTERNS

There were those times when Mack Bolan had the eerie feeling that things were in the saddle and riding mankind—as Emerson had once observed—and this was one of those times.

The thing had all gone so perfectly on the numbers, and it was pulling together with such symmetry and harmony, it almost seemed as though the *event* possessed an existence of its own and that it reached out to command time and *life* to give birth to itself, to *become*—and that the thing itself, the *event* was stronger and more important—and even more real— than any or all of the people involved.

There she sat, an old river derelict, squatting in a watery grave and brooding over her past with all the presence of any gaudy lady who had outlived all her loves, and all her beauty, and even all her excuses for living. The laughter "up east" had probably been justified: the *Jubilee* was clearly beyond redemption. The telltale sags and bulges in her wooden structure spoke not of cosmetic needs but of basic organic rot, of advanced old age which could not be reversed, of a terminal illness which sought only final peace.

But the *Jubilee* had been quite a gaudy lady in her day. She had shared a time and a people which and who had become immortalized with the river itself in song and sonnet. The "old man river" himself went rolling along, sure, eternally—but the water itself, made anew daily, was not the river and it was not eternal. Beds and banks and clustered molecules did not a river make. *Things* made rivers and boats *and* people—and history itself. Things *were* eternal. And, yes, dammit—things rode mankind.

Which was okay with Bolan. Somehow the idea provided a pattern to the mysteries of life and even a reason for all the pains as well as the satisfactions.

Patterns there were, for sure.

Toni was the first one down. She ran into his arms with a whoop and a wriggle, and he swung her clear around in the jubilant embrace. She was wearing sharp red slacks and a crushed velvet top, she looked great and none the worse for the wear of the day, and Bolan could only send a thanks to that "somewhere" in the universe where patterns were made.

"Where've you been while all the work was going down?" he asked her, in mock reproval.

"Frolicking," she replied, cocking her head and showing him the full-charm smile. "Boating, my deah, along the levee Riviera—at the hulk club, y'know—the most *charming* view of the scrap yards and all the chic salvage places."

A beaming older brother straightened the report out in his own version of plain English: "What a lucky strike, Sarge. Right down the pike all the way. Artie's boys brought her here, okay—and, say, wait 'til you see inside. You said a scrap heap—it's worse than that. Six sick termites could finish the thing off."

166

Toni soberly reported, "Mr. Giamba was very nice to me, very gentlemanly. I had the free run of the boat, long as I didn't try to chew through my leash."

Bolan told her, "You're here. That's all that counts."

"Sorry about the flub, commander."

There was nothing needing an apology, but she seemed bound to do it, so he let her run.

"He's an old faker. I thought he was unconscious. I took a bath—a very quick bath. But it was long enough for the old faker to find the telephone and send for help."

"It's okay," Bolan said. "Worked out fine."

"Sure did. Gave me a lot of free time for sober reflection. And in the quietness of my sobriety, I ratified our little discussion of the morning—yours and mine, I mean. Scared sick, bound hand and foot, monstrous rats running around in plain and audacious view—with all that, Mack, my decision remained unshaken. I'm where I choose to be."

Good for her. Not everybody Bolan knew could make that statement. "Then you're lucky," he told her.

"What's this all about?" Pol asked.

"Heaven and hell," Toni brightly told him.

The big brother bucked his head and raised his eyebrows in a soft dismissal of all that. "Oh. Able Group."

The others were straggling out, moving slowly along the rickety gangway to the levee. A motley group, almost pathetic when you considered the force they'd decided to stand against. Twenty men at the most, and only two or three of these less than fifty years of age. "Businessmen," these—not professional guns. Not, of course, that they were not dangerous men. These guys had survived some savage competitions in their day.

Artie and Jules came along the gangway together. The old *don* seemed not nearly so frail in his working clothes, but he was moving with care.

The two paused on the levee beside Bolan and

looked him up and down. Then Giamba said, "Don't know why you're doin' this. Don't really care why. I just think it's one for the books. You got my thanks whether you got 'em coming or not."

Bolan told him, "Save your thanks, Artie. I could be coming back for you some day."

"You better hurry, wiseguy. Unless you're better than the angels."

"I've never challenged heaven, Artie."

"Just hell, eh?"

"That's right."

The old man gave him a final brush with the eyes and went on.

Vino Jules nodded his head and passed silently.

Tony Dalton was close behind.

"You didn't get very far south," Bolan commented, remembering the guy from the junkyard.

"You can't make it stick," the guy said, the eyes worried. "There'll be another Ciglia next week."

This one was young enough, but he was no wolf. Bolan told him, "I can only start it, Dalton. You'll have to make it stick."

"Me?"

"You can't leave it to them," Bolan said, his gaze flicking after the exhausted old men. "Challenge hell, guy."

Dalton looked him up and down—growled, "Thanks, maybe I will"—and went on.

Bolan watched the entire procession by, nodding impassively here and there at a familiar face, then he told Blancanales, "The numbers are probably plenty tight. I expect Ciglia will be here at first dark—but I can't really depend on that. I can't spare you here, Pol, but we do need a forward scout. I guess you're elected for that."

The Pol had to agree with that. "I guess this will work okay," he added, critically surveying the site.

168

"I'd like to set the old hulk adrift," Bolan mused. "Make the boarding parties have to work for it. But we can't let it get out into the shipping channel, and I doubt there's any way to control it."

Blancanales shook his head at that. "Might even come apart before we want it to. She's got anchors, but the chain looks bad. I wouldn't risk it."

Bolan sighed. "So we risk the other. I see Ciglia as an organization man. He'll come from every side—by land *and* by sea. It has to come just right. I want them all here together. I want an absolute Cong High."

"What is that Cong High?" Toni asked brightly.

Blancanales absently told her, "Little thing we picked up in 'Nam—the hard way."

"It's a type of ambush, Toni," Bolan explained. "Most of the action at the center, a folding operation on the sides."

"Like scooping up a bunch of fish in a net," Pol added.

She wrinkled her nose. "I wouldn't be much help with that, I guess. I'll be your scout."

Bolan's gaze ran from the girl to Pol and back to the girl again. "Okay. Take the blue Chevy. It's wired and gassed, keys are in it." A vision of her flashed through his mind, a single-frame still of a cornered but spitting young lady on a big lake near New Orleans, and he grinned with that memory. "Weapons, too, but you'd better not get into that. Ride them low and break off as soon as you have their intentions. Keep in radio contact but keep it brief and guarded. You're Blue Star, we're North Star."

"I know that game," she said. She hung a light kiss on each of them and walked away to the Chevy.

"There is a gal," Blancanales declared fondly.

"And a half," Bolan added to that measure. "Okay," he said, quickly jerking his mind back into the grim business at hand. "We'd better get it moving. Is Gadgets working his wonders?"

"Oh yeah. You know Gadgets. Every damn hair has to be in place. He does set a sweet stage, though, doesn't he? You think we have until first dark, eh?"

The Bolan gaze went reflexively to the skies. The pattern, yeah. Light, dark, shades of gray. This one would go down in darkness.

"First dark, Pol," he replied grimly.

It always came, finally, to the darkness.

22: CONG HIGH

"What the *hell* are you doing here?" the skipper yelled at his battered intelligence chief.

"They needed the bed," Postum explained with a feeble smile. "Or hadn't you noticed the blood on our streets lately?"

"You look terrible! Get out of here!"

"Just stopped by on the way home, Skipper. Few things to pick up. Uh, I thought—is it okay with you if I run the vacation in right behind the sick leave? I've been promising Janice and the kids that trip to the Caribbean for three years now."

The skipper was giving him that "come, now!" look. Postum had been collecting pay in lieu of vacation since he'd joined the force. He'd *never* had a vacation.

"Seriously," the intelligence chief insisted. "What's wrong? Why are you looking at me like that?"

"Nothing." The skipper waved his hand in dismissal.

"Sure, it's okay. Get out of here. Go home and go to bed."

Which was precisely what Postum had in mind. But then the hot line beeped and the watch commander's announcement changed that. "Code contacts, Skipper. Same bunch, with a new wrinkle. They've added a female."

"ADF report!" the skipper snarled.

"Negative. ADF overwhelmed. Widely scattered sources, transmissions too brief to fix."

The skipper stormed out of there.

Postum grinned understandingly and followed at a more leisurely pace, the new rate of movement not entirely dictated by the trussed-up leg.

He reached the bull room just as a monitor crackled with one of those "briefs." A new, female wrinkle, yeah—crisp and businesslike.

"Ten out and still rolling them."

The voice, responding: *"Firm the count. Watch for splits."*

On a different monitor, then, the soft voice: *"What is the make?"*

The Chicano: *"Cong low."*

Bolan: *"Cong low and running east. Count ten and building."*

Back to the other channel, the female: *"There is a split. There is a split."*

"Count!"

"Five east, ten north. That is a tally and wrap it!"

"Break off north! Track east!"

"What the *hell* are they saying?" the skipper fumed.

"Damned if I know," Postum murmured, though guessing silently.

"Can't you get me a sector isolation?" the skipper yelled at the communications technician.

"Negative. Signals are diffused, widespread."

Postum pulled up a chair, sighed, and sat down. The

skipper strode to the window and stared into the quickening nightfall.

From the monitors, then, the soft voice: *"I have no make."*

"Cong low," the taut voice of Bolan advised him.

"Cong low,"' the Chicano echoed.

The skipper kicked the wall.

Postum grinned, reached into his pocket for a cigarette—the first in years—lit up, sat back, and enjoyed.

It sounded like a fun game. Tom Postum knew that it was not.

The digital clock on the communications console rolled on. The skipper paced and the commtech stared at his monitor dials. Tom Postum smoked.

Then, the female again, the signal stronger now, peaking into the red on that monitor dial: *"Levee Riviera with a better view. This is a final."*

Bolan: *"Great work! Break off! Rejoin North Star!"*

North Star, huh? Postum mused. Nice name for an RV. Very symbolic, too.

He could picture the benign face of "Gadgets," poised intently above that Flash Gordon command console as the soft tones drifted through the monitor: *"Cong high east. I have acquisition."*

"Cong low north," reported "Pol."

"Watch the folds," Bolan urged. *"Get them all high. We want no lows."*

"I'm getting a fix," the commtech reported. "Preliminary indication is Sector Four."

"Back *there* again?" the skipper asked unbelievingly.

"It is a preliminary. Stand by. We will fix the next transmission."

It came a moment later, from the Chicano: *"Cong north."*

"Watch for a north split to low!" Bolan cautioned.

"Affirmative, I have a split. Call it all congs low north, scratch and repeat."

173

"Realign, realign! North Star is east! Ground Star is south! Red Star is west! Report congs!"

From the RV, then: *"Cong high east and centering."*

From the Chicano: *"Cong low south but moving."*

From Bolan himself: *"Cong low west and rising. Close it in! Fold it!"*

The skipper fumed, "What's this cong high, cong low stuff? Tom? What is it?"

Postum silently shook his head. It was an echo from Vietnam, sure, but an echo which only certain specialties would understand. Fun games, no. It was the *grim* game.

"ADF fix!" the commtech excitedly reported. The wall was lighting up. The alarms were going down. Men were running.

Tom Postum sighed, went to his office, and began gathering his stuff for the long vacation ahead.

Hell.

These damn cops didn't stand a chance against those soldiers.

They were coming in, and they were coming hard, and that was good. It was precisely what Bolan had banked on. He had not underestimated Jerry Ciglia. A quiet word in an alert ear was all it took in this business. It had been enough for Ciglia. No beating the bushes for this one, no sending out scouts—no furtive actions whatever which may tip the hand and flush the pigeons from the sure-thing slaughter pen.

Ciglia was coming for heads, and he meant to have them.

Five crews had transferred to two swift power launches and were moving upriver to seal off any possible river escape.

Another five were rolling inland and coming in across the delta while the other five rolled in across the top in a pincers movement.

The big overkill.

But a perfect set for the Cong High game.

Bolan had been patrolling the inland approaches in the Corvette. He'd made the quiet contact, tracked the play into the kill zone, then stashed the little car and closed on foot for the grand finale.

Blancanales was out there on the levee, just lying out there, about a hundred meters off center.

Schwarz was in the warwagon and cruising the flanks, confirming the readings, preparing to come in finally as the big-punch sealant.

And "the camp" was ready for victims.

The old triple-decker had been dolled up just a bit in that brief time allotted for the "set." Kerosene lanterns were strung along the open decks at strategic points, others glowing feebly behind cabin windows on the two main cabin decks. The windows of the salon had been draped in black and a congregation of lanterns placed in there.

Schwarz's special touch added the final notes of realism—a collection of small cassette recorders loaded with tapes of actual bugged conversations and strewn around into various cabins on continuous playback.

Quiet music was coming from the salon and the muted buzz of quiet conversations issued from all over that old hulk.

Yeah . . . a perfect set for the Cong High kill.

And they were slipping in higher and higher by each suspenseful moment. The two big launches were laying-off out there in the darkness, engines idling and barely audible even to Bolan's expert ear. The cars had been ditched somewhere in the background and the gunners were making the final overland approach on foot—coming in from every angle.

From Bolan's quiet drop in the bushes, he spotted a group of three in a running crouch moving quietly across the cement levee to the south, then another three at the other end—all disappearing into the shadow of the *Jubilee*—reappearing a moment later clambering hand over hand up the side to the top deck.

An engine on the river revved slightly—and Bolan knew what was going down out there, also.

His thumb was poised above the ignition button on the black box as he waited them all in—but there was, of course, a moment of diminishing returns of which he must remain cognizant. If those early boarders should tumble to the setup and give the alarm, the whole thing could fall to hell quicker than a remote button could trigger a Cong High party.

The stealthy movements on the river side were becoming more and more prominent and the levee boarders seemed to be without end.

These boys were greedy.

As greedy as Bolan—and they were playing as quiet a game—getting all the headmen on board and stealthily placed throughout the old cruise boat before making the final move.

Bolan was rewarded for his patience when he caught a movement on the upper deck, a figure moving awkwardly out of the shadow of the pilot house—moving awkwardly because of a "turned ankle" and limping along with a cane.

The moment had arrived. The "chairman" would be among the last to board. Those who were left out were meant to be left out—and the Cong High plan took that sort of caution into account.

Regret punched that button—regret not for the actors upon that stage but for the stage itself, for the final end to a romantic past—regret for the last gallant fling of the gaudy lady.

She blew in a series of trumpeting explosions, beginning below-deck and working upward in a wave motion that scattered blowtorch flames and flying fire-brands in a panoramic sweep of the entire kill zone.

Human figures hurtled outward and crumpled to the levee or plunged into the big muddy. Startled screams and agonized shrieks superimposed themselves upon the thundering tumult of high explosives in sudden destruct.

But the gaudy lady went without a groan of her own—her decks quietly folding and falling, her bulkheads powdering and scattering into the eternal flow of old man river, her once comfortable cabins puffing into quiet flames and releasing themselves to the atmospheres for the quiet trek back to a romantic past.

And down upon the levee, the levee so low, a sturdy Cong High veteran with a combat-ready machine gun was blowing a staccato accompaniment to the old girl's swan song, catching the "low congs" in their startled desire for disengagement.

A flaming motor launch drifted into Bolan's line of sight while another roared away in a power surge to nowhere.

"Nowhere" because that was where the flaming arrow from "somewhere" hurtled across those tortured skies to intercept and discourage any further independent movement. One moment the launch was there and powering into a classy turnaround, the next it was not.

Frightened men were scurrying across the delta, shouting words of comfort back and forth—headed not to the front but to the rear—but there were not many of these, and Bolan let them go. This particular kill needed witnesses for maximum mission effect.

The physical effect was certainly there, in all its grim reality.

As the tall man in black strode along the levee toward his partner, he snatched the black box from his belt, spat on it, and hurled it into the grave of the St. Louis Corporation.

"There you go," he muttered. "All you crazy bastards. Welcome out of my world."

An "idea" had found its natural end.

And now, *this* old man was rolling home.

EPILOGUE

Able Group plus One were all in the warwagon and rolling silently along the levee in a quiet tactical withdrawal long before the grim young men of the police tactical squads reached the astounding scene of action.

"Anything to debrief?" Schwarz asked, peering owlishly back at the group just before the farewells were due.

"Nothing here," Bolan reported. He was slumped tiredly in the ready seat, making notes in a leather-covered black book. "Oh, except . . . be sure to take your cut from the Stonehenge bank. Throw a fourth of the net into the war chest. Take the rest."

"That's too much," Pol argued. "We're here on fees, anyway."

"That guy couldn't pay you enough for *that* job," Bolan insisted. "Take the money. It just weights me down." He raised a steady gaze to the sturdy fellow. "I couldn't pay you enough, either," he added solemnly.

"Don't embarrass me, Sarge."

Bolan was still staring at him. "Talk to your man yet?"

"Yeah." Pol grinned sourly. "He's delighted. And the lady is even more delighted that he's retiring from politics."

"That's sine-logic for you," Schwartz commented sorrowfully.

"Aw, shut up, dammit," Pol said softly with a grin at Bolan.

"Where do you go from here, Mack?" Toni asked, with just a bit of high color in her cheeks.

"Home," he said quietly.

"Oh. I guess I'd forgotten you had one."

"So had I. I got reminded. Toni ... it's been great seeing you again. It's never long enough, is it. We'll uh, connect again. Somewhere. Won't we?"

"I have a feeling we will," she replied, sighing.

They made the switch at the Gateway Arch. The farewells were tough and quick, almost brutal—then three of Bolan's favorite people were fading away into the night.

He drove on to the airport motel, put the big bus in a ready-out park, showered, donned fresh clothes, and rejoined that other world for a brief respite from hell.

He ran into Leo Turrin in the lobby. The little guy was pacing tracks in the carpet and viciously chomping a cigar. He reacted to the sight of Bolan with a relieved scowl and hurried to intercept him.

"I got a seat on the nine-thirty plane," he announced with some agitation. "Johnny's in the room, watching TV. I was wondering if you were coming straight back."

"You mean if at all, don't you?" Bolan corrected him.

"Okay, so I worry a little," Turrin replied with a sour smile.

"Why the hot jump home, Leo? I told you I might take twenty-four hours."

"I found out different. That's why the hot jump. My boss got called to New York for a hot council, and no one's home tending the territory. Seems they got some disturbing news, about a half-hour ago. They're saying that Little Artie whacked out Jerry Ciglia and all his legions. That was stunning news, I guess."

Bolan just stared at him.

"Well, dammit?"

"Well, dammit," Bolan said soberly, "you better hurry if you expect to catch that plane."

"You're not going to tell me, are you! You're just going to let me stew about it all the way home!"

Bolan said, "It's true, Leo. Ciglia went storming out to an old boat called the *Jubilee* to collect some heads. I guess you never heard of the *Jubilee*. Me either. Anyway, Ciglia got collected, instead."

"And? So?"

"Read about it in the papers, guy. I have no time for stories from hell. I have to go watch a kid become a man."

He winked at his best friend in any world, spun on his toe, and went to keep that date in paradise.

It would, he knew, be his very last.

The End

THE INCREDIBLE ACTION PACKED SERIES

DEATH MERCHANT

by Joseph Rosenberger

His name is Richard Camellion, he's a master of disguise, deception and destruction. He does what the CIA and FBI cannot do. They call him THE DEATH MERCHANT!

Order		Title	Book #	Price
_____	# 1	THE DEATH MERCHANT	P751	$1.25
_____	# 2	OPERATION OVERKILL	P085	.95
_____	# 3	THE PSYCHOTRON PLOT	P641	$1.25
_____	# 4	CHINESE CONSPIRACY	P168	.95
_____	# 5	SATAN STRIKE	P182	.95
_____	# 6	ALBANIAN CONNECTION	P670	$1.25
_____	# 7	CASTRO FILE	P264	.95
_____	# 8	BILLIONAIRE MISSION	P339	.95
_____	# 9	THE LASER WAR	P594	$1.25
_____	#10	THE MAINLINE PLOT	P473	$1.25
_____	#11	MANHATTAN WIPEOUT	P561	$1.25
_____	#12	THE KGB FRAME	P642	$1.25
_____	#13	THE MATO GROSSO HORROR	P705	$1.25

TO ORDER

Please check the space next to the book/s you want, send this order form together with your check or money order, include the price of the book/s and 25¢ for handling and mailing, to:

PINNACLE BOOKS, INC. / P.O. Box 4347
Grand Central Station/New York, N.Y. 10017

☐ CHECK HERE IF YOU WANT A FREE CATALOG.

I have enclosed $_____ check_____ or money order_____ as payment in full. No C.O.D.'s.

Name_____

Address_____

City_____ State_____ Zip_____
(Please allow time for delivery.)